The Other Woman

Lois Lane sighed and tried to relax. But she was filled with too much anxiety, too much curiosity.

Whatever Clark Kent was up to, he was going to have to level with her. After all, they were engaged. She had a right to know.

"You say something?" the cabbie asked, glancing at her in the rearview mirror.

"No," said Lois, realizing with some embarrassment that she'd been expressing her thoughts out loud. "Nothing at all."

Biting her lower lip, Lois shook her head, then turned and looked out the side window at the passing buildings. Whatever else happened tonight, she vowed that she would find out *exactly* what was going on between Clark and Janna Leighton.

Look for these

novels

Heat Wave
Exile
Deadly Games

From HarperPaperbacks

ATTENTION: ORGANIZATIONS AND CORPORATIONS

Most HarperPaperbacks are available at special quantity discounts
for bulk purchases for sales promotions, premiums, or fund-raising.
For information, please call or write:
Special Markets Department, HarperCollins*Publishers***,**
10 East 53rd Street, New York, N.Y. 10022.
Telephone: (212) 207-7528. Fax: (212) 207-7222.

DEADLY GAMES

by M. J. Friedman

HarperPaperbacks
A Division of HarperCollinsPublishers

If you purchased this book without a cover, you should be aware that this book is stolen property. It was reported as "unsold and destroyed" to the publisher and neither the author nor the publisher has received any payment for this "stripped book."

This is a work of fiction. The characters, incidents, and dialogues are products of the author's imagination and are not to be construed as real. Any resemblance to actual events or persons, living or dead, is entirely coincidental.

HarperPaperbacks   *A Division of* HarperCollins*Publishers*
10 East 53rd Street, New York, N.Y. 10022

Copyright © 1996 DC Comics. All Rights Reserved.
SUPERMAN, LOIS & CLARK, and all related elements are the property of DC Comics.

Superman created by Jerry Siegel and Joe Shuster.

No part of this book may be used or reproduced in any manner whatsoever without written permission of the publisher, except in the case of brief quotations embodied in critical articles and reviews. For information address DC Comics-Licensed Publishing, 1700 Broadway, New York, N.Y. 10019.

First printing: June 1996

Printed in the United States of America

HarperPaperbacks and colophon are trademarks of HarperCollins*Publishers*

❖ 10 9 8 7 6 5 4 3 2 1

For Roger Zelazny,
creature of light

Acknowledgments

The author would like to recognize the efforts of Rick Hautala, without whose hard work and diligence this book would not have been possible. Thanks are also due to Mike Carlin, KC Carlson, and Mike McAvennie at DC Comics, for invaluable noodling. Finally, the author would like to express his gratitude to Charles Kochman, Ann Goetz, and Scott Sonneborn—for giving me this project in the first place, and for displaying exemplary dedication and care throughout the course of the creative process.

1

LOIS LANE COULDN'T STOP staring out the oval window beside her seat. The jet taking her back to Metropolis was skimming over a mighty terrain of clouds, complete with cliffs and canyons and strangely shaped crags.

Though she couldn't see the sun itself, it was setting somewhere up ahead, just starting to turn the edges of the clouds pink and amber. Here and there were specks of fiery red.

If Lois squinted, she could almost imagine a blue-and-red blur, breaking through the solid cloud bank and streaking upward to meet her. A blur that was faster than a speeding bullet, able to leap tall buildings in a single bound . . .

She watched as her breath fogged over the window and then faded away. "Clark," she whispered softly.

It wasn't entirely out of the realm of possibility that he would come flying by. After all, Clark Kent knew what flight Lois was on. It wouldn't have been all that difficult to find her plane and give her an unexpected welcome home.

She whispered again, "I've missed you, Superman."

Still, with her fiancé's superhearing, even a whisper was clearly audible—that is, if he was listening for it.

"What's that, dearie?"

The sudden voice beside her startled Lois. She turned toward the plump, gray-haired woman who had been sitting beside her since the jet left Paris early that afternoon.

Even in first class, there wasn't all that much elbow room. And throughout the flight, this woman had managed to take up most of it with her knitting supplies.

Not that Lois had complained, of course; she had better manners than that. But right now she craved some space. Even a casual conversation seemed like a nuisance.

"Hmm?" Lois said.

"I thought you said something about a *super* man," the woman replied.

Her face wrinkled as she smiled at Lois, exposing enormous white teeth. The overhead light reflected from her blue eyes, making them glisten like ice.

Lois chuckled a bit nervously. "Oh, no . . . it was nothing. I was just thinking out loud," she said.

"Well, you know," the woman went on, "if you want to meet a *really* super man, I could introduce you to my grandson, Bobby. He's going to meet me at the airport when we land, you know."

Lois nodded politely. "Yes, I know. You mentioned that." Maybe a dozen times, in fact, since they left Paris.

"Did I mention that he sells—"

"Life insurance," Lois interrupted, despite herself. "In Tulsa. You already told me."

The woman nodded. "And he's *very* successful at it, I might add. While you were looking out the window and daydreaming, I found that photograph of him that I was looking for."

She thrust her hand forward, practically pushing the small snapshot into Lois's face. Lois knew that it would be rude not to at least glance at it.

The faded photograph had obviously been taken some years ago. It showed a fresh-scrubbed young man wearing clothes that had since gone out of style. Bobby *was* rather handsome, Lois had to admit to herself, but not nearly as handsome as Clark Kent.

"He looks . . . very nice," she said, smiling. "But as I told you, I'm already engaged."

Just then, thankfully, the intercom came on. The captain's mellow voice drew everyone's attention.

"This is Captain Richards. We'll be landing at Metropolis Airport in just over an hour. The weather in Metropolis is sunny with temperatures in the low to mideighties . . . "

"Well," the old woman said, still smiling widely as she tucked the photograph back into her purse, "I think I'll go freshen up."

Watching the woman head toward the restroom, Lois sighed with relief. She felt even better when she saw someone else enter the restroom first. That would give her a little more time before her neighbor came back.

Time to be by herself. To look forward to seeing Clark again, after having been away for an entire week. Time to come to grips with her feelings over going to Paris without him.

Not that it had been her fault. Not really.

The *Daily Planet* could only afford to send one reporter to interview Howard Marsten, the wealthy Metropolis shipyard owner and boat-builder who had sold off all his investments and retired to France. Almost overnight, it seemed, he had become a prominent and respected artist.

People in Metropolis were eager to know more about Marsten's metamorphosis. And since this was the first interview the man had granted since he left the country, Lois would have been a fool not to go.

And one thing no one could call Lois Lane was a fool.

This was a scoop she couldn't pass up, period. Even if it meant being away from Clark for a while.

Besides, Lois thought, she would find a way to make it up to him. She considered calling Martha Kent and asking for the recipe to one of Clark's favorite dishes. Not that Lois was any great cook, but she could give it a shot.

Despite her jet lag, she would invite Clark over tonight and make his favorite dinner. Better yet, she'd make it a candlelight meal—with a bottle of champagne.

No, she cautioned herself. *Champagne comes from France. Why rub it in?*

Lois watched as her travel companion entered the restroom. As soon as the door closed, Lois grabbed the cellular phone from the compartment in front of her and punched in her calling card code, followed by the private number of Perry White, managing editor of the *Daily Planet*.

On the third ring, she heard her boss pick up the other end. "White here," he snapped.

Lois smiled, amused that she would find Perry's gruff voice actually welcoming. No place like home and all that, she thought.

"Hi, Chief, it's Lois. I'm just calling to make sure my faxes came through all right."

"Everything came through just fine," Perry said. "Terrific piece, by the way. And the answer to your next question is *yes.* Of course we're going to make it the feature in tomorrow's edition."

"Great," Lois said. Perry could read her like a book.

She glanced up and saw her neighbor just leaving the restroom. She knew she had to hurry if she was going to say everything she wanted to with some degree of privacy.

"Is Clark there? I'd like to—"

"Not now, Lois. Looks like I've got a little emergency on my hands. Gotta go—see ya in the morning."

The line clicked and went dead.

"Sure thing, Chief," she replied, as if there were someone still there to hear her.

Lois frowned slightly as she replaced the phone. A moment later the old woman returned and slipped in beside her.

She had freshened up, all right. The scent of her flowery perfume was overwhelming. Lois turned and looked back out the window.

Was it just her imagination, she wondered, or was Perry being evasive for some reason? Her reporter's instincts told her that something was going on.

Could Clark be upset with me? she wondered. *Maybe even jealous that I went to Paris for a week without him?* Was that what Perry was trying to hide?

It wasn't like Clark to give in to petty emotions. But men were such strange creatures—who knew?

Lois smiled suddenly, almost hoping that Clark really *was* a little miffed at her. It would make it that much more fun to make up with him.

Gazing out the window again, Lois noticed huge holes in the cloud terrain and sunlit patches of land far below. The shadows of clouds shifted across the dizzying vista.

She tried to imagine that one of those shadows was moving faster than the others—faster even than the jet she was in.

"Bobby will be there when we land," the old woman said. She had the expression of a used-car salesman trying to seal a deal. "I could introduce you to him, if you'd like."

Lois turned to the old woman. "Unfortunately," she said, "I've got someone coming to meet me."

The woman looked at her. "Oh. Your . . . fiancé, I suppose?"

Lois nodded. "That's right. But thanks anyway."

It seemed to take forever, but eventually the intercom started to chime, and the bright red *FASTEN SEAT BELTS* signs winked on.

Lois's stomach did a little flip as the jet banked around into its approach pattern. The sun had already set. The strobe landing lights flashed like fireflies on the runway far below.

She was still staring out the window as the plane shuddered under the influence of a head-wind and made contact with the tarmac. The engines roared as the plane decelerated, shifting Lois forward against her seat belt.

Not the smoothest landing, Lois told herself. But having flown into the upper reaches of the atmosphere in the arms of the man she loved, so high that she could see the entire planet, she could never again be rattled by anything that happened in a 747.

Even before the plane stopped and the *FASTEN SEAT BELTS* signs were turned off, relieved chatter and nervous laughter filled the cabin. The passengers crowded into the aisles and fetched their carry-on luggage from the overhead compartments.

Lois listened to the bustle in the plane, but she couldn't make her getaway with everyone else. The old woman next to her didn't look too eager to fight the crowds; she was just sitting there.

Lois didn't want to inconvenience the woman, so she sat back and made the best of it. Heck, she hadn't seen Clark in a week. Another few minutes would only heighten the anticipation.

She waited until the woman had started toward the door before getting up and retrieving her own luggage. Finally, with both pieces in hand, Lois exited the plane and followed the enclosed ramp to International Arrivals.

After passing through Customs and Immigration, Lois walked out into the expansive waiting area. The lights were so bright they stung her eyes. The room was crowded with passengers coming and going.

She looked around for Clark, smiling despite herself. But he was nowhere to be seen.

"Where *is* he?" she whispered to herself.

A cold, sinking feeling filled her stomach. He was all right, wasn't he? Had something happened to him that Perry hadn't told her about? Had something happened that Perry didn't even *know* about?

Outside Lois could see that night had fallen. The airport windows looked like huge slabs of black marble, reflecting the bright lights inside the terminal.

All around her the crowd hurried along. She

heard squeals of delight as friends and family greeted one another. She watched enviously as people hugged and shook hands, happy to see each other at journey's end.

But no Clark.

Gritting her teeth and tightening her grip on the handles of her carry-on luggage, she started toward the escalator.

"Hey, Lois!"

The reporter jumped when she heard her name, but she knew immediately that it wasn't Clark who had called her. She forced herself to smile as she turned and saw Jimmy Olsen pushing his way through the crowd.

Jimmy was carrying his camera, as usual. After all, one never knew when a "photo-op" would present itself.

"Did you have a nice vacation?" he asked, smiling broadly as he gave her a hug and took her luggage.

"It wasn't a vacation," Lois replied, smirking at his sarcasm, "and you know it. It was work, smart alec." She craned her neck and looked around. "Where's Clark?"

Jimmy's cheeks turned dark red. For the briefest moment he pursed his lips and looked away.

First Perry, now Jimmy. Something is definitely going on, Lois mused.

"Um," said Jimmy, "Clark's not here. He got called away."

"Called away?" Lois echoed, a little peeved.

After all, she'd been gone for a whole week. The least the man could do was come get her at the airport. "Called away by *whom*?"

Jimmy gave her a crooked smile and shrugged. Clearly he knew more than he was saying. And with Jimmy, it was just a matter of time before she pried it out of him.

They walked along, allowing the press of the crowd to move them toward the escalator. Neither one said anything as they started down to the first level and began the long walk over to the luggage carousel.

But Lois was burning with curiosity—especially since she hadn't gotten a chance to speak with Clark in person the last few days. It had been difficult to hook up with him, what with the time difference and their busy schedules.

But she had left messages on his answering machine, reminding Clark when her flight arrived and telling him how eager she was to see him again. There was no way he could have forgotten.

"Is this your young man?"

Lois recognized her traveling companion's voice. Turning, she saw the elderly woman trundling along to catch up. Beside her was a tall young man with dark hair and sparkling blue eyes.

That would be Bobby, Lois thought. She had to admit that he looked even better in person than in his photograph.

Lois glanced quickly at Jimmy, then shook her head. "No, my . . . er, young man was called away.

On business. This is a friend of mine, Jimmy Olsen, from the *Daily Planet*."

"The *Daily Planet*? You don't say," the old woman said. "Well, this is my grandson, Bobby—"

"That's Robert," the young man said, reaching to shake Lois's hand. "Robert Hancock."

His grip was warm and strong, but certainly not as strong as . . . someone else's, Lois thought.

As Robert smiled, he displayed the same huge white teeth his grandmother had. Lois almost laughed out loud, imagining having children with such large teeth.

"You're Lois Lane," Robert said. "I recognize you from your picture in the newspaper."

"I've heard so much about you," Lois told him. "It's nice to finally meet you in person."

"Gram and I were going to catch a cab into town and go to Balducci's for dinner." Robert tilted his head. "Would you and your friend care to join us?"

Lois didn't have to consider it for even a second. She smiled as she said, "Oh, I'd love to, but I really do have to meet my—"

Robert's grandmother made a clucking sound with her tongue. "What's this world coming to when a man will leave a woman stranded like this?"

"It was a pleasure to meet you," Lois said, addressing both the old woman and Robert.

She tried her best to smile but felt it wasn't very convincing as she wheeled around and confronted Jimmy. "Okay," she said, changing the subject and trying her best to control her frustrated curiosity. "I want you to tell me—right now—just what in blazes is going on here!"

He sighed. "Okay. But I don't think you're going to like it."

"Try me," she told him. Anything was better than remaining in the dark.

At least that's what she thought.

TRYING NOT TO BE TOO OBVIOUS, Clark Kent used his X-ray vision to peek through his jacket sleeve at his wristwatch. He frowned. It was already a little after seven.

Damn, he thought, feeling a wave of guilt. Lois's plane would have landed by now—and he had promised to meet her at the airport. At least Jimmy would be there.

Sighing, he glanced around at the busy dining area. The soft glow of candlelight illuminated the smiling faces of well-dressed patrons. Speakers strategically placed throughout the large, elegant room supplied the soft strains of Vivaldi's *Four Seasons*.

Without a doubt, he thought, the Cossack Tea Room was the ritziest restaurant in all of Metropolis.

Night after night, the place was filled with the sounds of hushed conversation and the clink of fine silverware against china plates. Waiters and waitresses smiled as they hurried about, the soles of their shoes whispering softly on the plush carpet. Tourists and locals alike gawked at the celebrities they might see dining here.

Or at least, that's what he'd heard. It wasn't as if Clark could afford to come here very often—not on a reporter's salary. But then, tonight he wasn't footing the bill.

Clark sat back and felt the gentle give of the thick, leathery upholstery. Sitting next to him, despite the ample size of the booth, was a woman about his own age—in her mid-to-late twenties.

Janna Leighton, heiress to the Leighton megafortune. And, more to the point at this particular moment, a very beautiful woman.

The candlelight caught the highlights of her long blonde hair. It flashed in her emerald-green eyes.

"Oh, what's the matter now?" Janna asked.

"Er . . . nothing," Clark replied.

She shot him a look of skepticism, then leaned forward and covered his hand with hers. Her touch was surprisingly warm.

"Come on," Janna said. "You could at least *act* like you're enjoying yourself."

Ever so gently, Clark withdrew his hand from her grasp. But he couldn't help being aware of how close she was. Or how tantalizing he found her perfume.

He shifted uneasily in his seat. The leather padding made a soft creak that sounded almost like someone groaning.

"I'm fine," he assured her.

"Sure you are," she told him, obviously not believing him for a second. "I hope you're not thinking about . . . *her*."

"About whom?" Clark replied, feigning innocence.

"You know who I mean," Janna said. "Lois Lane. You're not thinking about her, are you?"

Clark shrugged. "Of course I am."

The heiress shook her head disapprovingly. "Well, I don't think you should feel the least bit guilty about this. After all, *she* didn't hesitate for a moment to leave you and fly off to Paris to spend a week with the notorious Howard Marsten." She arched an eyebrow. "Until he retired, Marsten was one of the richest men in Metropolis, you know. Well, after my—"

Her voice caught ever so slightly before she finished.

"—my father."

"Lois isn't like that," he said.

Janna tilted her head. "I hate to tell you this, Clark, but *everyone*—"

Clark never heard the end of her sentence. A sudden motion off to his left drew his attention. Turning quickly, he saw that something was wrong.

A swarthy, heavyset man wearing a dark suit was making his way toward their table. Even indoors, the man was wearing a hat pulled down low over his brow.

Clark knew immediately that the newcomer was neither a waiter nor a celebrity hunter. There was a mean, dangerous look in the man's eyes, which didn't blink or shift the least bit as he approached Clark and Janna.

Instantly Clark scanned the newcomer, using his X-ray vision. Through the man's jacket, he saw a nine-millimeter pistol in a shoulder holster. The man's right hand was moving, ever so slowly and steadily, up and inside his coat.

He's going for his gun, Clark thought.

There was no time for him to change into Superman. Quickly he noted a waiter carrying a tray full of hot soup a few steps behind the gunman.

Angling himself so Janna couldn't see what he was doing, Clark shot a concentrated burst of his superbreath in the direction of the waiter. The breeze caught the leading edge of the tray, tilting it backward.

When the waiter tried to adjust for the sudden shift of weight, he lost his balance and tripped over his own feet. With a loud cry, he toppled forward.

The soup shot into the air just as the intruder brought his hand out from inside his coat. Clark could see him holding the gun now—and raising it to aim at Clark's companion.

For a split second, the soup seemed to hang suspended in the air. Then, like a dark tidal wave, it splashed over the man's back, shoulder, and gun hand.

As the scalding liquid made contact with his skin, the gunman howled so loudly his voice drowned out the other sounds in the vicinity—the clatter of breaking bowls and falling silverware and the exclamations of a frustrated, surprised waiter.

The intruder bent over, his face contorted with pain. His suit coat was steaming. Thick, chunky soup dripped onto the carpeted floor.

But more importantly, the man had dropped the gun.

The patrons sitting closest reacted to the sudden flurry of activity. In the scuffle of feet, Clark saw the gun get kicked under a nearby table.

Seeing his chance, he made a dive for the gun, but the press of the panicked crowd blocked him. The gunman, obviously realizing his window of opportunity had slammed shut, turned and dashed for the front door. As he ran, he swung his elbows and fists wildly, knocking aside anyone in his way.

Clark thought of searing the doorknob with his heat vision, making the handle too hot to touch. But the frenzied swarm of fleeing patrons blocked his view of the door, and he couldn't take a chance on hurting anyone.

Janna was lying facedown on the seat, her hands covering her head. Realizing that she had momentarily lost track of him, Clark seized the moment and took off down the corridor to the nearby men's room.

Fortunately the restroom was empty. In a flash, Clark changed into his alter ego.

Effortlessly Superman raised the wire-mesh window over the sink and struck out into the night. In less than a second, he had zipped around to the front of the restaurant.

The line of people waiting to get in was taken aback as the gunman, bellowing in pain and anger, raced past them. No one on the outside was sure of what had happened inside, so no effort was made to pursue him.

Flying just above the sidewalk, Superman followed the disarmed gunman as he fled down the street. The man's footsteps clicked loudly on the pavement. He had his head down and was running toward a dark alleyway when the Man of Steel landed several paces in front of him.

The gunman almost ran into him. At the last possible moment, he came up short. Panting hard, he glared at Superman.

"You might as well come quietly," the Man of Steel advised him.

He stood there with his hands on his hips. A soft breeze caught the edge of his red cape.

"No!" the man bellowed. "Get out of my way!" He made a fist of his unburned hand and shook it threateningly.

"That burn looks pretty serious," Superman said mildly. "You might need to have it checked at the hospital before you go to jail."

The gunman didn't hesitate for an instant. Grunting, he lunged forward and threw a wild punch at his adversary.

There was a lot of strength behind the punch.

But the man's fist bounced off Superman's chest as if he had struck an iron wall.

Clutching his hand to his chest, the gunman howled in pain. He seemed to have forgotten about the injury to his other hand.

"You're only going to make it worse," Superman noted. "I can guarantee that you broke a couple of knuckles just then."

The man's face was twisted with rage as he made a fist with his left hand, stepped in, and swung again. This time Superman took a quick step backward. The punch whistled harmlessly through the air in front of him.

Superman didn't have time for games. The uproar in the restaurant would die down quickly, and he didn't want his companion—or anyone else—to notice he was missing.

Stepping forward, he found a pressure point where the man's neck met his shoulder. He squeezed ever so carefully.

The man groaned, his eyes rolled back in his head, and his knees gave out from under him. He started to fall, but Superman scooped him up before he could hit the pavement.

"I guess some people just don't know when to stop," the Man of Steel remarked, as he flew with the gunman back to the front of the Cossack Tea Room.

A squad car with its lights flashing and siren wailing had just pulled up to the sidewalk. Two policemen leaped out of the cruiser and were making their way toward the restaurant when

Superman landed in front of them with the unconscious gunman in his arms.

"He's all yours," he announced, handing the man over to the astounded patrolmen. Without another word, Superman turned and leaped into the air.

Luckily no one had thought to hide in the restroom, so it was still empty when Superman flew back in through the window. Changing quickly into his civilian clothes, he dashed into the dining area and, adjusting his glasses, blended into the chaos as best he could.

Glancing in Janna's direction, Clark saw that she was sitting up in the booth, brushing her hair from her face as she looked around at the commotion. Dropping down onto the floor, he crawled on his hands and knees to the table where he had last seen the gun.

He found it. Then, trying his best to look bewildered, Clark stood up and brushed himself off with one hand as though just emerging from the protection of the table.

"*There* you are!" Janna shouted to him.

He walked over to the booth. Leaping up from her seat, Janna hugged him tightly and gave him a big kiss on the cheek. As gently as he could, Clark broke off the embrace and took a step back.

"And look at this!" the heiress said, pointing excitedly to the weapon in Clark's hand. "You got his gun!"

Just then the two policemen burst into the restaurant. Not wanting any trouble, Clark gingerly placed the gun on the table before they saw him with it.

"No, I, uh . . . it was just lying there on the floor," he said. "So I picked it up." He shrugged.

"Don't be so modest," the young woman told him, smiling brightly. "I saw what you did. Why, Superman himself couldn't have done a better job of protecting me."

"You don't say," Clark replied, letting one side of his mouth curl into a crooked smile.

"Oh, but I *do* say," Janna insisted, tilting her head as she gazed at Clark. "Lois Lane's loss is definitely *my* gain."

In a suite at the Metropolis Arms, the bearded man heard the phone ring. Glancing at his associates, he crossed the room and picked up the receiver.

"Yes?" he said.

The voice on the other end was not a happy one. "It didn't work."

The bearded man suppressed his anger. Apparently, this would not be as simple an operation as he had hoped.

"We are not done yet," he told the man on the other end of the line. "Is our other option in place?"

"It is," the other man confirmed.

The bearded one nodded. "Then we may yet make this evening a success."

With that, he hung up the phone. Crossing the room again, he took his seat.

And waited.

3

EMPTY PARKING SPACES were at a premium, and it took Jimmy a long time to find a place where even his compact car could fit. It was still quite a distance from where he and Lois Lane wanted to go, but it was the closest they could get.

Lois got out on the passenger's side and met Jimmy on the curb. A noisy crowd was streaming around them, all heading in the same direction.

There were already hundreds, possibly thousands of people ahead of them in the night, and more were coming all the time. They were all gathering in the plaza in front of the antique brick facade of Metropolis Stadium.

Street vendors wended their way through the assemblage, loudly hawking hot dogs, cold drinks, pretzels, T-shirts, souvenir pennants, and Metropolis Monarchs baseball hats. Exhaust fumes from passing cars and buses mixed with the aroma of fast food that hung like mist in the warm spring air.

Looking around, Lois noticed several structures across the street from the stadium, each covered with a series of thick, multicolored tarpaulins. The corners of the tarps flapped lazily in the breeze.

"Gosh, I leave the country for one week, and look what happens," she said.

Of course she'd known about the construction hereabouts. She knew that the Monarchs were planning something big. But she hadn't followed events closely enough to know what was to be announced today, or by whom.

Nor would she have come here with Jimmy instead of going straight home from the airport if he hadn't told her Clark would be here. She had decided that she wanted to see this with her own eyes.

At the moment, Jimmy had two thirty-five-millimeter cameras draped around his neck—one with a telephoto lens, the other with a wide angle. As always, he was ready to get all the shots he needed for the *Planet*.

By showing their press credentials, Lois and Jimmy gained access to the press aisle. They fell in step with the stream of other media people, all carrying video cameras and spotlights or some kind of recording device. All the local TV stations had vans parked nearby for live news feeds back to the station.

Lois and Jimmy followed the push of the crowd. Finally they stopped in the roped-off area in front of a large makeshift stage that had been erected by the stadium's main entrance.

The sudden glare of spotlights trained on the stage made Lois blink. It took a few moments for her eyes to adjust to the brightness. She noticed a podium bristling with microphones and a row of folding chairs behind it. Other than that, the stage was bare.

Suddenly a trumpet fanfare blasted out over the numerous loudspeakers that had been set up around the stage. The echo of the music rolled away into the night until it was drowned out by cheers and whistles.

Lois watched along with the crowd as two white stretch limousines started slowly down the street toward the stadium. Dozens of policemen pushed the crowd back to let the limos go by.

A strange nervousness coiled up inside Lois's stomach as the cars pulled to a stop in front of the stage. Flashbulbs popped when the doors of the first car opened and Mayor Berkowitz stepped out. He was followed by several other city officials and the Metropolis Monarchs' front-office personnel.

Cheers and a few stray catcalls greeted the city officials as they walked up onto the stage and sat down. Lois watched the door of the second limousine open.

An even bigger explosion of flashbulbs went off as Janna Leighton stepped out. Lois frowned.

Janna was the heiress to Leighton Industries. Just a few months ago, her father had passed away, leaving her his financial empire, conservatively estimated at half a billion dollars.

That empire included a lot of profitable companies in a variety of growing industries, not just in Metropolis but all over the world. But the gem in the crown of Leighton Industries had always been the Metropolis Monarchs baseball team. That was the enterprise of which Old Man Leighton had been the proudest.

The crowd cheered again as Janna, smiling broadly, turned and waved to them. Lois hated to admit it, but the woman looked gorgeous.

She was dressed in a dark blue evening gown with silver sequins that sparkled like tiny exploding stars. Her long blonde hair wafted like a cloud around her face and shoulders. Still smiling, she turned toward the carpeted stairs that led up the stage.

Well, Lois thought sourly, *here it is*. The moment of truth.

The limousine door was still open. As she watched, Clark slid out. Hooking her arm through his, Janna allowed him to escort her onto the stage.

Moving across it with all the poise and confidence in the world, the heiress stopped and smiled at Clark—his signal to release her arm. Then she took her position at the podium and squinted into the glare of spotlights and popping flashbulbs.

All the while, Lois's gaze was fixed on Clark.

She watched as he walked to the back of the makeshift stage and stopped in the shadow of a stadium support post. Folding his arms across his chest, he waited for Janna to begin.

So did everyone else. The crowd hushed in anticipation of what she had to say.

But Lois was more concerned with the figure in the background—the man who just happened to be her fiancé. The man who had passed up the chance to see her at the airport, after a week of forced absence, in order to escort Janna Leighton to . . . to *this*.

There had to be an explanation, she told herself. And it had darned well better be a good one.

Suddenly Clark's expression changed—to one of surprise and concern. Looking around, it took him only a second or two to find her in the crowd.

Their eyes met. And though she couldn't see Clark quite as closely as he could see her, she couldn't mistake his look of helplessness. It seemed to her he wanted to speak with her, to explain—but under the circumstances, of course he couldn't.

The question was . . . why not? What was he doing up there on that stage, instead of down here with the other reporters? If Jimmy's information was accurate, what was it about Janna Leighton that had kept Clark at her side the last few days?

Apparently those answers wouldn't be immediately forthcoming—at least not until this little shindig was over.

Janna leaned forward and gripped the edges of the podium. She surveyed the crowd, the spotlights reflecting off the sequins on her gown.

"Good evening to you all, and welcome," she said, speaking into the microphones with the full enthusiasm of a cheerleader. Her amplified voice reverberated and rebounded from the stadium and the neighboring buildings.

"As many of you already know, my father, Alexander Leighton, president of Leighton Industries and owner of the Metropolis Monarchs, passed away earlier this year. At that time he left me in charge of all his business interests. My father was well-known for his charitable works and for his contributions to the community—to the entire city of Metropolis . . . "

Well, not exactly, Lois thought.

Alexander Leighton had hardly been a model of community spirit. As owner of several city blocks surrounding Metropolis Stadium, he had been cited time and again for negligence vis-à-vis his responsibilities as a landlord.

In fact, he'd never given anything to anyone unless it was financially prudent to do so. That was true not only in Metropolis, where his holdings were immense, but everywhere else in the shadow of the Leighton empire.

The crowd, however, was too caught up in the excitement of the event to dispute Janna's remarks. They listened raptly, even those who might have suffered as a result of her father's indifference.

"I made a promise," the heiress went on, "to my

father on his deathbed—a promise that I would not only continue with his good works, but that I would expand upon them."

She made a quick hand flourish—a signal. The huge spotlights that lined the top of the stadium suddenly swung around to light up one of the concealed structures across the street.

Even Lois turned, intrigued by what was going to come next. For the moment, at least, her other questions were placed on the back burner.

Janna beamed. "My professors in college always taught me that it is very good business to take care of the neighborhoods where you *do* business. With that in mind, I'm unveiling here tonight the first of what I hope—no, what I *know*—will be many gifts from Leighton Industries to the wonderful people of Metropolis."

On cue, the tarpaulins fell away from the structure Janna had indicated. The crowd let out a collective gasp at the marvelous steel and glass building revealed to them in its finished form for the first time. Only a few months ago, there had been nothing there but dirt and debris.

"This is a brand-new fitness center for the people of Metropolis," the heiress announced. "The first small step in what I am determined will be the largest act of urban renewal in the history of this wonderful city."

The crowd exploded with enthusiasm. The microphones began to wail with ear-piercing feedback until someone turned down the volume.

"Starting tomorrow," she said, "every citizen of

Metropolis is invited to come in and register to be a member of this facility. And the best part of it is, it's absolutely free. All you have to do to become a member is sign up."

Lois couldn't help staring at the new fitness center. It stood out from the rest of the tenement-ridden neighborhood, a shining atoll of prosperity in a sea of poverty and despair.

Even a few moments ago, when Lois had heard Janna's promises to benefit this area, she had had her doubts. She had to admit now that maybe she had been wrong in her skepticism.

"This is just the first tiny step," Janna said. "Over the next several days and weeks," she went on, indicating the other concealed structures with a sweeping gesture, "We intend to open a number of other facilities. And I intend to publicize their unveilings with a series of celebrity competitions, all of which will be televised. The proceeds from these events—one hundred percent of them—will be used to fund food banks, child care facilities, and shelters for Metropolis's homeless."

Out of the corner of her eye, Lois thought she saw someone move. Turning, she looked for Clark on the platform.

He was no longer standing there in the shadows. He was gone.

That usually meant only one thing. There was a job for Superman somewhere. If that was true, Clark hadn't totally lost sight of his responsibilities. But under the circumstances, that was cold comfort for Lois.

Janna, meanwhile, was working the crowd. "This is my way of saying thank you, Metropolis." She clenched her fists and waved her arms above her head. Flashbulbs exploded in the night like blasts of early summer lightning.

"Thank you from me and from my father for all the wonderful, wonderful support you've given us, Leighton Industries, and the Metropolis Monarchs over the years. And now . . . "

She paused dramatically and turned toward the back of the stage.

"I want to introduce this year's team. Ladies and gentlemen. I present to you . . . the *Metropolis Monarchs* . . . "

As the crowd applauded, the Monarchs trotted out onto the stage in their still-spotless home uniforms and lined up behind Janna.

"It's going to be a *terrific* year to play ball," she laughed.

THE THICKSET MAN KNEELING in front of the open window braced the high-powered rifle against the hollow of his shoulder. He was in a vacant apartment on the top floor of an abandoned building, directly across the street from Metropolis Stadium.

Squinting his left eye shut, he brought his right eye up to the magnifying rifle scope and focused on the street below. A multitude of bright lights made it look like daylight on the street. Through the open window, he could hear Janna Leighton's voice, echoing from the loudspeakers surrounding the stage.

The man took a short, shallow breath. He moved the rifle and scope around until the dark crosshairs were lined up perfectly on Janna

Leighton's forehead. He could see the bright emerald-green of her eyes.

"Too bad to waste such a pretty face," the man whispered. He snickered to himself as he brushed his forefinger lightly, almost lovingly, against the curved metal of the trigger.

He had no regrets about what he was about to do. All he had to think about was how much he was being paid for the job, and—for all he cared— it could be his own grandmother there in his gun sights.

With such powerful magnification, it was impossible to keep the scope absolutely steady, but the assassin had no doubt he could do the job with one clean shot. That's why he had been hired as backup, in case the first attempt at the Cossack Tea Room tonight failed.

And apparently it had.

The man had his escape route planned to the fraction of a second. All he had to do was pull the trigger and get out as fast as he could.

Shortly thereafter, he would dump the rifle—he already knew where. After that, it would be a simple task to lose himself in the crowd until he got away.

Slowly and steadily, he started to apply pressure to the trigger. A hot thrill of excitement coursed through him, making him feel momentarily light-headed. He always felt like this just before a shoot. He loved the feeling.

Suddenly, though, his view of Janna Leighton blurred.

Without taking his eye from the scope, the gunman thumbed the adjustment knob, trying to bring his target back into focus. He let out a short, sharp gasp when, through the scope, he saw a close-up view of a huge red *S* against a yellow background.

"What the—?" the man sputtered.

His finger automatically jerked back on the trigger. There was a sharp explosion as the rifle kicked back in his hands, so hard he almost dropped it.

The man heard a high, whining sound as the bullet ricocheted in the room. By the time it was still, the sniper knew what had happened.

It was red and blue and hovering outside his window, looking not at all pleased. Trembling with fear, the sniper lowered his rifle and stared, amazed, at Superman.

"How did you—?" he blurted. "What am I doing? I've got to get out of here."

Dropping the rifle to the floor, the sniper turned and started to run. In a flash, Superman flew past the man and was standing in front of him, blocking his escape route.

"Bad idea," the Man of Steel told him. He looked angry. "A *very* bad idea."

The last thing the gunman saw before blacking out was a bright white light that exploded across his vision. And then . . . nothing.

With a soft punch to the jaw, Superman knocked the sniper out cold. Then he caught the man before he could hit the floor.

He knew that he could easily fly down to the street and deliver the unconscious sniper to one of the policemen working on crowd control, but he had his reasons for not wanting anyone to see him. Instead he propped the man up so he was leaning against the wall, his legs splayed awkwardly in front of him.

Picking up the rifle, Superman twisted the metal barrel around the unconscious man's arms. He had already checked the rest of the area outside with his supervision and superhearing, so he knew there were no other threats to Janna Leighton . . . at least, not right now.

Once Janna's speech was finished, he expected her to take off whether he was with her or not. He had left her instructions to that effect earlier on.

Looking around, Superman saw the assassin's jacket hanging on an exposed nail in the wall. A cellular phone stuck out of one pocket. Silently thanking the man for his helpfulness, the Man of Steel took out the phone and dialed the Metropolis Police Department.

When the dispatcher answered, he identified himself and asked for a couple of patrolmen to come up to the apartment. He also requested that whoever responded to his call do their best to be discreet. He informed the dispatcher that there had been an attempt on Janna Leighton's life, and that he didn't want her or anyone else in the crowd to know anything about it.

Waiting for the police to arrive, Superman walked over to the window and looked down at

Lois. It bothered him deeply to see her searching the stage, a troubled expression on her face. He knew she was looking for him, wondering why he was acting so strangely.

Once again he felt a pang of remorse for not meeting her at the airport as she had expected him to. Unfortunately, he'd had other obligations, which he couldn't drop, no matter what.

What's more, he still had those other obligations. No matter how Lois might feel about it, he had to keep on doing what he was doing.

When he heard the footsteps of the patrolmen coming up the stairway, Superman checked to make sure the gunman was still unconscious, then leaped through the open window and flew away.

Saving lives was often the easiest part of what he did. Unfortunately, the hardest part was still ahead.

Lois turned when she saw Jimmy making his way toward her through the crowd. She had been so intent on the new fitness center, then on Clark's whereabouts, that she hadn't even seen the photographer slip off.

Judging from his expression, however, Jimmy hadn't been idle. He slapped his camera case with the flat of his hand.

"I knocked off seven rolls," he said, grinning with satisfaction. "Got some great shots, too."

"I'm sure Perry will be pleased," Lois noted absently.

She could see that Clark hadn't returned, and

she couldn't help wondering where he—or Superman—had gone. If there had been trouble nearby, she was sure she would have seen him.

Or would she?

"That was some speech, don't you think?" Jimmy asked.

Lois nodded. "It's easy to make promises, though. Let's see how she follows through with them."

Jimmy frowned. He didn't say anything, but Lois could tell he thought she was being less than charitable.

"I mean," she continued, "it isn't as though her father was the saint she makes him out to be. Right?"

"Yeah . . . right," Jimmy replied.

Lois bit her lip. "You think I'm being catty, don't you?"

The photographer shrugged. "Under the circumstances, I guess I understand why. But like I told you before, I'm *sure* Clark has a—"

"—a good reason for spending so much time with her," Lois said, finishing his sentence for him.

She sighed. No doubt Clark had a perfectly *fine* explanation.

And truth to tell, maybe she *was* being a little catty. It was one thing for a reporter to embrace a healthy skepticism and another to doubt what seemed like genuine altruism.

By then, Lois was watching Janna and the city officials get back into their limousines. Thankfully, Clark was still nowhere to be seen—a situation that didn't seem to bother the heiress at all.

That made Lois wonder. Was it possible she had

guessed where Clark had gone—just as Lois herself once had? But that would mean that Clark had told her he was Super—

No, thought Lois. *Impossible.* Clark had waited until he proposed to admit his secret to her. There was no way he would reveal it to a woman he barely knew.

And despite everything, Lois was sure he barely knew Janna. The reporter wouldn't convict him until she'd seen all the evidence. Or anyway, she'd *try* not to.

The crowd parted as the limousines started up and drove away into the night. Jimmy smiled.

"I, uh, I suppose you want to go home now, huh?" he asked.

Lois looked at him and tried to smile back but couldn't. She knew she had no reason to be angry with Jimmy. After all, *he* hadn't done anything wrong except try to skirt the issue of Clark and Janna back at the airport.

It wasn't his fault that her fiancé had spent the last few days with a beautiful heiress. Or that Clark hadn't provided Jimmy with a reason for his actions.

Lois took a deep breath and, for the first time since getting off the plane, felt the fatigue of her transatlantic trip. Setting her jaw, she made up her mind.

"I was wondering if you could do me a little favor," she said.

Jimmy's expression said that he'd go to the moon for her. But then, he was that kind of guy.

"What's the favor?" he inquired.

"Would you drop my luggage off at my place?"

Before Jimmy could say yes or no, Lois fished her keys from her purse and pulled her spare apartment key off the ring.

"I'll catch a cab later," she said. "There's . . . someone I have to go see."

"Someone we both know pretty well?" he prodded.

"That's right."

Jimmy nodded. "No problem. And good luck."

"Thanks," she told him.

Lois handed him the key. Then she started looking around for a cab, knowing they'd be few and far between once the crowd petered out.

Catching a glimpse of something big and yellow, she turned to see a taxi round the corner. Hailing it before anyone else could, she waited until it stopped and then slid in.

"Where to?" asked the cabbie, an older man with a thick mustache and glasses.

"Three-forty-four Clinton," she said.

That was Clark's address. He was bound to be there by now—or shortly.

Hell, she thought, *he'd* better *be there*.

"You got it," the man told her, and pulled away from the curb.

Sinking into the upholstery, Lois sighed and tried to relax. But she was filled with too much anxiety, too much curiosity.

Whatever Clark was up to, he was going to have to level with her. After all, they were engaged. She had a right to know.

"You say something?" the cabbie asked, glancing at her in the rearview mirror.

"No," said Lois, realizing with some embarrassment that she'd been expressing her thoughts out loud. "Nothing at all."

Biting her lower lip, Lois shook her head, then turned and looked out the side window at the passing buildings. Whatever else happened tonight, she vowed that she would find out *exactly* what was going on between Clark and Janna Leighton.

5

CLARK FLEW THROUGH the window of his apartment in a blur of red and blue and changed out of his costume. Then he called Janna Leighton. She answered from the phone in her limousine.

"Everything all right?" he asked.

"Clark! Where did you run off to, exactly?"

"I was, um... checking out something suspicious."

"You're sweet to try to protect me," Janna told him, "but you've done enough in that department. That's what the police are there for."

"I guess," he said.

Of course he couldn't tell her about his efforts as Superman, or how all the police protection in the world wouldn't have saved her if he hadn't caught the assassin in time.

"You know," Janna went on, "if you keep trying to be a hero, you'll get yourself hurt. And that's the last thing I'd want to see."

"Yes," he said. "I know. Well, I'm going to call it a night. See you tomorrow, then?"

"I wouldn't have it any other way," she replied. "Pleasant dreams, Mr. Kent."

"Good night," he said, and hung up the phone.

He had started to call Lois when he heard the sound of footsteps outside his front door. He didn't need to use his X-ray vision to know who it was. He hung up the phone.

Before Lois could knock, Clark opened the door and took her in his arms. Picking her up with a hug, he carried her into the apartment and shut the door behind him.

After all, he hadn't seen her in a week. He had missed her.

Lois was so taken aback, she responded in kind. That is, until she had a moment to think. Then she withdrew.

As Clark looked into her angry eyes, he sighed. He should have known it wasn't going to be that simple.

Lois's first reaction on seeing Clark was to hug him just as hard as he was hugging her. It was the natural response of someone in love. And she would have continued to respond that way, except for what she had seen and heard in the last few hours since her return to Metropolis.

Pushing him away abruptly, Lois tried to get a

grip on her emotions—but it wasn't easy. "Oh," she said, "so *now* you're glad to see me."

"I'm *always* glad to see you," Clark told her earnestly.

Lois frowned. "But not so glad you'd want to be there to pick me up at the airport. Or miss out on a date with some heiress."

Lois could tell by Clark's expression that he was feeling very uneasy. *Good*, she thought. It served him right.

"I'd say you owe me an explanation," she added.

Clark nodded. "I'd say the same thing, if I were in your place. Unfortunately . . . I'm afraid I can't give you one."

Lois had been prepared for a wide range of excuses. But no excuse at all? Not even an *attempt* at one?

He shrugged. "I know it sounds lame, Lois. And believe me, I'd like to set your mind at ease. But you're going to have to trust me on this one—I just can't."

She looked at him. "Why not?"

Clark pressed his lips together. "I can't tell you that, either."

Lois nodded, more than a little perturbed. "I get it. You spend the evening escorting Janna Leighton, whom *some* people consider a beautiful woman. But are you covering the event like a good reporter? No, you've somehow become one of her entourage. Worse, it turns out you've been at her side almost constantly for the last few days, while your fiancée was working her tail off a continent away.

"And when that same fiancée asks you *why* you've been doing this, you tell her you'd *like* to give her an answer—you just can't." She grunted. "Tell me, Clark, why would I have trouble accepting that response?"

He held his hands out, helpless. "I'm not interested in Janna Leighton, if that's what you think. That's not it at all."

"Of course not," she replied. "That's why you walked up onto that stage arm in arm with her. That's why you and she have been such an item lately."

Clark opened his mouth as if to say something, but stopped himself. Turning away from her, he shook his head.

"Sorry," he said at last. "I know how it looks. But it's not that way."

Lois wanted to believe him. Clark had never lied to her before, in all the time they had known each other. Of course, he had covered up his identity as Superman, but that was before they fell in love. It didn't really count.

All right, she told herself. *I'll give him another chance.*

"Whatever the reason you were with Janna Leighton tonight, I'll understand. I just want *you* to trust *me*," she said. "Because no matter how bad it is, it'll be easier for me to take than being left in the dark."

Clark looked back over his shoulder at her. He seemed torn, though she couldn't tell exactly why.

"I . . . can't," he answered.

Lois felt her heart sink. "You *can't*? Or you *won't*?"

He turned to her again. "Please, Lois. I know we're . . . we're partners and all, and . . . and much more than that. But you're asking me for something I just can't give you."

Lois stared at Clark, hurt beyond words. If he couldn't confide in her, if he couldn't let her in on this, no matter what it was . . . how secure could their relationship be?

"All right," Lois said softly, unable to keep the disappointment out of her voice. "If that's the way you want it . . . "

Turning quickly, she reached for the door and opened it. Then she looked back.

Clark was standing in the center of the room, his face a mask of anguish. There was no doubt about it—this was every bit as painful for him as it was for her.

But that didn't make Lois feel any better. It didn't solve anything.

"Bye," she told him.

He looked at her. "Lois . . . "

Ignoring him, she started down the hall toward the elevator. After all, what was left for them to say to each other? Clark had a secret he didn't want to divulge, and that was that.

Reaching the elevator, Lois got in and pressed the button for the lobby. As the doors closed, she could still hear Clark's voice in her head, pleading with her for understanding—though he wouldn't give her the least little insight into the reasons for his secrecy.

In any case, she knew one thing—Clark wasn't falling in love with Janna Leighton. If he were, he would simply have told her so. He wouldn't have tried to hide it behind a veil of secrecy.

No, there was something more going on here. Something she couldn't even begin to guess at. Something that piqued her curiosity.

Lois heard the *bing* that told her she had reached the lobby. As the doors opened, she was still lost in thought—so lost, in fact, that she failed to notice the half dozen people waiting outside.

"Aren't you getting off, ma'am?" a man in a jogging suit asked politely.

Realizing that they were waiting for her, Lois blushed. "Yes, thank you," she muttered, and exited the elevator.

As she brushed past the small crowd and eyed the door of the building, she knew what she had to do. She was a reporter, after all. She would get to the bottom of this despite Clark.

And she *would* get to the bottom of this, Lois promised herself as she walked outside into the warm spring night. Clark didn't stand a chance of keeping a secret from her.

6

LOIS WALKED INTO THE city room at the *Daily Planet* at 8:00 A.M., and already the place was noisy with ringing telephones and clacking keyboards. The graveyard shift was just finishing up.

Without pausing to greet anyone, she made a beeline for Perry White's office. Arriving at his half-opened door, she poked her head in.

As usual, his sleeves were rolled up. He looked up from behind his desk.

"Morning, Lois. Good to see you back."

"Morning. Can we talk?" Lois asked.

Perry nodded and gestured for her to come in. Pouncing on the invitation, she entered the office and closed the door behind her. Immediately the city room din became something distant and tolerable.

"What can I do for you?" the editor asked.

On Perry's desk, Lois could see the morning edition of the paper, hot off the presses. Her interview with Howard Marsten and her byline were emblazoned across the bottom of the page, along with a file photo of the former shipbuilder.

Lois couldn't deny feeling a slight thrill of pride, but she quickly shook it off. Her work in Paris was yesterday's news. Right now she had another agenda to pursue.

"Lois?" Perry prodded.

She straightened. "Excuse me, Chief. I was hoping you could tell me what's going on with Clark."

Perry grunted and leaned back in his chair, his brow furrowing. "I'd be glad to," he told her. "That is, if I knew anything worth telling."

Lois sighed. She had hoped that Clark was on some kind of secret assignment. But if even Perry didn't know about it . . .

"He hasn't told you anything?" she asked. "Anything at all?"

Perry looked at her. "I take it he hasn't told you anything either?"

She shook her head. "Not a thing."

The editor harrumphed and folded his arms across his chest. "Well, then," he said, "all I can say is *this*—a few days ago, Clark came to me with an idea about doing a profile on Janna Leighton. You know, background stuff. With this brouhaha at the stadium coming up, it seemed like a good idea, so I gave him the go-ahead."

Lois leaned forward. "Then what?"

Perry shrugged. "Something happened. All of a sudden, he was on to a much bigger story. At least, that's the impression he gave me. But Clark couldn't give me any details. He wanted me to trust him—to give him the freedom to pursue it—without knowing anything about it." He chuckled. "And I said yes."

"Just like that?" she said.

He nodded. "By my lights, Clark's earned a little leeway. I would've done the same thing for you, Lois, if something similar came up. You know that."

She believed him. But it didn't help her much right now. Lois had been hoping for a lead of some kind—something to send her in the right direction—but it was clear her boss didn't have the answers she was looking for. She was going to have to get them from someone else.

Perry's expression became sympathetic. "Look, Lois. If you want to work on the more public story of Janna Leighton's contributions to Metropolis, then go right ahead. Bring Jimmy along to get some pictures, in fact. Have a ball." His voice grew firm. "But whatever you do, I don't want you poking your nose in Clark's story. Understand?"

Lois began to protest, but Perry held up a hand to stop her.

"I mean it," he said. "If this is as big as Clark hinted it was, I don't want anybody getting in his way—not even *you*."

She bit her lip. Perry knew what kind of reporter she was. Under normal circumstances, she wouldn't let anyone—not even Superman—get between her and a story.

But these weren't normal circumstances, were they? Besides, she couldn't disobey a direct order from her editor.

"Lois . . ." Perry said gruffly.

"All right," she told him. "I promise I won't get in his way."

He smiled. "Good. Now get going."

Lois did as she was told. As she closed the door to Perry's office behind her, she was already trying to think of a fresh angle on Janna's public crusade.

Not that she'd forgotten about Clark, or his little mystery. But if she could find out more about Janna, she might find out more about what Clark was up to as well.

As Clark, at Janna's side, entered the brand-new outdoor roller skating rink, he couldn't help being a little impressed. The place was everything she had said it would be.

The skating surface itself was a dark blue composite material, very smooth and apparently very durable. Tiny drains, actually slits less than a tenth the width of an in-line skate wheel, were built in to make sure there weren't any accumulations of water anywhere.

Brightly painted bleachers rose up and out from the skating surface on every side, already filling up with excited spectators and newspeople. At the far end of the rink was a small, Art

Deco–style building for skate fittings. After all, this was going to be a community facility, and a great many people didn't own their own skates.

Janna took Clark's arm in hers. "What do you think?" she asked.

He nodded approvingly. "Pretty nice."

After all, until recently this place had been little more than a garbage dump, a block away from the stadium.

"Nice?" she echoed, frowning. "That's *all* you can say?"

He smiled. "All right. It's gorgeous. And more importantly, it's going to be a big asset to the people who live here."

"That's better," said the heiress, smiling again.

She pulled Clark over to the center of the rink, where the contestants were pulling on their equipment while the track was being marked off. To commemorate the opening, Janna had arranged for a roller relay race—to be skated by a host of Metropolis celebrities.

Clark recognized several star players from the Metropolis Monarchs baseball team and the Metropolis Meteors football team. Mayor Berkowitz was there as well, smiling brightly as he chatted with the participants.

Clark also noticed some media personalities— among them Steve Lombard and Whitty Banter of WGBS-TV, the station that had paid to televise the event. There was also Clive Booker and Janita Holiday of WLEX-TV, and Olympic decathlete Nora Costello.

What's more, Janna herself would be taking part, despite the objections of the police. Whoever had made the earlier attempts on her life would be likely to try again, they reasoned—and unlike Clark, they didn't know the half of it.

He had objected, too, of course. But Janna insisted on going through with it.

After all, she was trying to make an impression on Metropolis with all her good works—trying to leave a legacy that would make people forget her father's unpleasant ways. And to her, that meant not backing off in the face of adversity.

Especially, she'd laughed, since she was such a good skater. It would be a pity, she'd insisted, to miss an event like this one.

Intent on ensuring Janna's welfare, Clark tipped his eyeglasses down and scanned the crowd using his X-ray vision. He didn't see anyone carrying a gun or any other weapon, and he hadn't heard anything threatening with his superhearing, but he knew that he couldn't relax.

The whole point of his being here—at least from Clark's point of view—was to keep the heiress safe. Of course, Janna didn't know that was part of his agenda—and he couldn't tell her without revealing that he was Superman.

As he finished his inspection, Clark saw Lois and Jimmy join the reporters in the media section of the bleachers. Unfortunately, he couldn't tell Lois any more today than he could yesterday. With luck, that would change, and soon—the sooner, the better, as far as he was concerned.

Feeling a hand on his arm, Clark turned. Janna was smiling at him. "Guess what? Mel Tonkin, the guy from WMET—he can't skate. He's got back trouble all of a sudden. That means we need a last-minute replacement."

Clark saw where she was going with this. "Janna, I can't—"

"Sure you can," she told him. "You skate—you told me so."

"But not very well," he maintained, concerned for his secret identity.

He didn't want to give anyone the impression that Clark Kent was a serious athlete, even if he could outrace a speeding bullet and bend steel in his bare hands. The more average he appeared, the less chance someone would suspect who he really was.

"You don't have to be good," Janna said. "We just need a warm body, and yours seems to qualify." Suddenly she turned to the other celebrities. "Right, everybody? Do we want Clark to skate? Or do we want to have to revamp the whole race?"

"Come on, Clark!" cheered Steve Lombard. "We need you, baby!"

"That's right," joked Whitty Banter. "You can't look any worse than me out there!"

Clark frowned. So much for his excuse of ineptitude.

Besides, he could just as easily watch over Janna on skates. As Superman, he had sometimes kept an eye on Metropolis at speeds that exceeded the sound barrier; it wouldn't be any hardship to do it while skating. And this way, he'd be able to scan the entire rink more closely.

"All right," he replied at last. "I'll do it. Just don't expect any miracles."

"Attaboy, Clark," called Will Paulson, third baseman for the Monarchs. "I knew you had it in you."

Nora Costello handed him a pile of equipment, including a red cotton vest with the Leighton corporate logo, a set of protective pads, and a white helmet. She winked at him.

"Welcome aboard, teammate."

He nodded to the decathlete. "Er, thanks."

"Don't embarrass us *too* badly," she said.

Clark smiled. "I'll try not to."

As he searched for his size in the collection of skates that had been provided, he saw Janna approach a standing microphone in the middle of the rink. She got some applause even before she started.

"Are you ready to have some fun?" the heiress cried.

Her amplified voice was loud enough to draw everyone's attention. The applause increased in volume.

"In that case," said Janna, "let the games begin!"

7

CLARK WAS STILL PUTTING on his pads when the starter's gun was fired. Almost everyone in the stands jumped at the sound. A little puff of blue smoke rose into the air, and the race was on.

There were five teams in all, each one set apart from the others by matching vests. Clark's team wore red, but there was also a blue team, a yellow team, a purple team, and a green one. Everyone wore a helmet, too, as well as elbow, knee, and wrist pads.

The rules were simple. Each skater was to negotiate two laps around the track and then pass the baton to the next skater. Of course, this wouldn't be a win-at-all-costs kind of competition. Good sportsmanship was more important.

Clark was racing third. He would hand the baton to Janna, who would skate the final two laps.

Watching from the sidelines, he saw that the green team had taken an early lead, though red—led by the Monarch center fielder—was a close second.

Nonetheless, he knew that he couldn't let himself get swept up in the excitement of the race. He had to keep an eye out for any signs of danger to Janna. A sniper could be hiding anywhere nearby—in a building across the street from the rink, on the other side of Hob's River, or even under the stands.

So far, though, everything looked fine.

As Clark watched the second group of skaters grab the batons from the first group, the red team was tied with the yellow for second, and green had a healthy lead. But before long, Nora Costello started to narrow the gap for the red team.

By the end of her first lap, she had pulled ahead of the green skater, a player for the Meteors who was a little too brawny to be all that fast. By the middle of Nora's second lap, she was well in the lead. Clark took his place on the track, knowing he would go next for the red team.

The crowd was getting more and more excited as the race went on, drowning out the grinding sound of the competitors' skates. One skater from the Meteors fell down and tripped up Clive Booker, but they helped each other up, brushed themselves off, and took off again.

As Clark positioned himself to receive the baton pass, he scanned the crowd one last time, satisfied that he didn't detect any potential trouble. Then Nora Costello approached him, skating as hard as she could and holding out her baton.

Even before he grabbed it, Clark was on the move. As Nora laid the baton in his hand, it took a bit of effort for him to hold back his superspeed and not just *zip* around the track. He knew he could go fast enough to set the composite on fire—literally.

After the first turn, Clark was gauging the strength of his movements and skating well, with long, fluid strides. But the Monarchs' second baseman, who was behind him, was catching up, slowly but surely—exactly as Clark had planned it.

Rounding the last curve on his first lap, Clark noticed someone lurking underneath the bleachers on the other side. Sensing danger, he poured on the speed, gradually widening his lead.

As he approached, he tried to get a better view of the person. But the crowd was on its feet now, making it difficult even with his X-ray vision. Everyone cheered as Janna took her position on the starting line, waiting for the baton pass from Clark.

He saw the heiress smiling at him as she started to move forward, pacing herself. Her hand was stretched out behind her, and she moved with a subtle grace. Despite Clark's preoccupation, the pass-off was perfect.

Feigning fatigue, he slowed and stopped along the side of the track. Bracing both hands on his knees, he leaned forward and pretended to pant,

Perry White (Lane Smith), Jimmy Olsen (Justin Whalin),
Lois Lane (Teri Hatcher), Clark Kent (Dean Cain),
Martha Kent (K Callan), Jonathan Kent (Eddie Jones).

though he wasn't even close to being winded. And all the while, he was looking for the person he'd glimpsed under the stands, knowing this might be yet another would-be assassin.

Then he saw who it was—and almost laughed. The mysterious figure was a guy named Fedders, whom Clark had interviewed once for a crime story. Far from being a danger to Janna, Fedders was obviously one of the officers assigned to look out for her.

Meanwhile, the anchor-leg skaters were coming into the last lap, giving it everything they had as the crowd urged them on. Clark couldn't help cheering for Janna.

But he wasn't so absorbed in the competition that he didn't see the yellow-team skater reach under his vest. By the time the man took out his gun, Clark had lowered his glasses. With his heat vision, he could melt the weapon, even at this distance.

Unfortunately the assassin was more resourceful than Clark had expected. A sudden stream of bright flames and sparks shot out from the man's heels, causing him to accelerate so fast he almost lost his balance in the turn.

Somehow he managed to stay on his feet. And with the extra speed, it took only a moment for the man to close the distance between him and Janna.

Worse, Clark couldn't see the gun anymore—it was hidden by the assassin's body. And as much as he wanted to keep the man from shooting Janna, he couldn't use his heat vision on the gun without going through the man.

That wasn't an option. Clark had promised himself long ago never to take a life, no matter what.

Instead he lowered his gaze and focused his heat vision on the assassin's footwear. Instantly the plastic and metal of the skates melted and fused together.

The man was moving so fast the jamming of his wheels sent him flying into the air. He looked like an awkward bird as he shot screaming over the skating rink railing, his arms and legs flailing wildly.

When he landed in the bleachers, the impact was hard enough to knock the gun from his hand. His skates sent up thick plumes of black smoke.

For a moment the crowd went silent, shocked by what they'd seen. Then a squad of plainclothes police converged on the impostor, making sure he didn't have any other tricks up his sleeve.

Despite the danger, Janna skated around the last turn and broke the tape that marked the finish line.

Clark was relieved. Janna had narrowly escaped death—yet again.

Watching from the stands, Lois and Jimmy saw a bunch of onlookers swarm over the errant skater. Lois hadn't figured it all out yet, but one thing was clear—the man had made an attempt on Janna Leighton's life.

And now that she thought about it, a couple of those "onlookers" seemed familiar to her. She smiled as she realized why. They were plainclothes cops whom she'd used as sources on more than one occasion.

So the police were here, staking the place out. Apparently they'd had an inkling something might happen.

Lois thought back to the night before, when Clark had disappeared. At the time, she'd imagined he was addressing a problem as Superman. Only now did it occur to her that someone might have been trying to pick off Janna Leighton.

"What do you think is going on?" asked Jimmy.

"Obviously, someone's trying to murder our Miss Leighton," Lois replied.

The photographer looked at her incredulously. "But what for?"

A good question, Lois conceded. A very good question.

For a moment she turned away from the action and looked at Clark. He was standing alongside Janna, looking as confused as everyone else.

Nonetheless, Lois reasoned, Clark was somehow responsible for foiling the gunman. The man hadn't just gone flying out of the rink all by himself. Clearly he'd had some help.

On a more personal note, she now had an inkling as to why Clark was spending so much time with the heiress. For reasons not yet clear to Lois, Janna needed protection of the sort only Superman could give.

But as Jimmy had asked, why would anyone want to kill Janna Leighton, especially now that she was making so many charitable contributions to Metropolis? And why wasn't Clark able to confide in her about it?

Obviously she would have to dig a little deeper for the answer to *that* question.

As the other newspeople rushed over to Janna, holding out their microphones for her comments on what had just happened, Lois became aware of something else: a thin, small voice, crying for help.

Looking around, she found the source of the cries—a teenaged girl, covering her mouth with one hand and pointing to a spot beneath the stands with the other.

Following the girl's gesture, Lois peered through the space between the bleacher seats and caught sight of a man in a skating outfit. He was slumped against one of the support pillars. His feet and arms were tied, and a gag of duct tape stretched across his mouth.

Lois tapped Jimmy on the shoulder to get his attention. "Down there," she said, pointing at the man.

The photographer instantly raised his camera and fired off a few shots. Then the two ran down the stairs together and around to the back of the stands.

The man was just regaining consciousness as Lois knelt beside him. She carefully pulled the gag away and loosened the ropes binding him. He groaned as he sucked in a deep breath.

It didn't take Lois long to recognize Danny Grove, the Monarchs' catcher. From behind her she saw several bright flashes of light and heard Jimmy's camera shutter click.

"What happened?" she asked.

Grove shook his head groggily as he looked up at Lois. He was obviously having trouble focusing.

"I—I'm not sure," he said weakly. "I was running late, coming back from my car with my skating gear, when I—I dunno." He winced as he reached up and rubbed the back of his head. "Someone must've conked me a good one from behind."

Lois grabbed her cellular phone from her purse and started to dial 911 to request an ambulance. But Grove put his hand over the phone.

"I'll be all right," he said, struggling to his feet.

"Are you sure?" Lois asked.

"I'm sure," he told her.

She folded up the phone and put it away. By then, she noticed, Jimmy had gotten all the pictures he needed.

"What's happening over there?" the catcher asked. With a nod, he indicated the crowd gathered at one end of the bleachers.

"I'm not sure," Lois told him, "but my guess is that's the guy who knocked you out and took your place in the race. The police have him now."

Before she could say any more, they were surrounded by uniformed policemen. Fortunately for Lois, the police were a lot more interested in Grove, who still had a pile of duct tape and rope at his feet, than they were in either her or Jimmy.

As the cops took charge of the situation, Lois grabbed her partner by the sleeve and led him out from under the bleachers. She had an idea, and she wanted to pursue it before the police did.

Jimmy looked at her. "Where are we going?" he asked.

"You'll see," she told him, "when we get there."

8

"NOW CAN YOU TELL ME where we're going?" Jimmy asked.

Lois made a left turn onto Bessolo Boulevard. For the hundredth time since they'd left the vicinity of Metropolis Stadium, she glanced in her rearview mirror.

All along, she had expected to see some evidence of the police. But so far, nothing. It seemed she was a step ahead of them—and the reporter in her was determined to stay that way.

"The man who tried to kill Janna Leighton was wearing some kind of rocket accelerators in his roller skates."

Jimmy nodded. "Uh-huh."

"Well," said Lois, "someone had to install those things."

"Okay."

"Well, there's a roller skating shop over on Fourth Avenue," she told Jimmy. "The owner's a man named Larry Cohen. He does a lot of customizing of ice skates and roller skates."

"That's right," said Jimmy. "You mentioned him in that article on the new Roller Derby team."

"Exactly. They get all their equipment from this guy."

Jimmy grunted. "But that doesn't mean he had anything to do with the gunman's skates."

"Maybe not," Lois agreed. "But it's a good place to start."

She felt a whole lot better now than she had just half an hour ago, before the aborted assassination attempt. Then she'd been at a loss, with no clear way to change the situation. Now she was in her element, on the trail of a hot lead—and if luck was with her, an equally hot story.

A couple of minutes later, she pulled to a stop in front of Skate Kraze on Fourth Avenue. To her satisfaction, there was still no sign of the police, plainclothes or otherwise.

The shop was small but modern, with a healthy assortment of skates and skating paraphernalia in ultraslick display fixtures. A small, wiry man with sparkling blue eyes and a gray handlebar mustache stood behind the counter. Lois recognized him as Larry Cohen, the owner.

Cohen grinned as he looked up from a skate he'd been tinkering with. "Good afternoon," he told them. "And how may I help you?"

Lois smiled pleasantly and identified herself. "I'm Lois Lane, from the *Daily Planet*. And this is Jimmy Olsen, my photographer."

The man snapped his fingers and nodded. "I thought I recognized you. You interviewed me when the Hornets came to town."

"That's right," Lois confirmed. "I was hoping I could ask you a few questions."

For just an instant, Cohen seemed to tense up. "Questions?" he echoed.

"We were at the celebrity skating race over by the stadium today," she began. Before she could say more, Cohen slapped his forehead.

"That's right," he said in a voice filled with disappointment. "I forgot the race was today. I wanted so much to be there."

He looked at her innocently—too innocently, Lois thought.

"How did it go?" the shop owner asked.

"It went just fine," she said. "That is, until someone tried to shoot Janna Leighton. Fortunately someone stopped him."

"Superman, I'll bet." Cohen nodded. "Gotta love that guy."

Lois shook her head. "Actually, it was the police."

Cohen grunted. "How about that. So no one was hurt?"

"Everyone's fine," Jimmy told him. "No casualties."

"Oh, good." The man took a breath and let it out, as if deeply relieved. "To tell you the truth, with Miss Leighton's announcement of a new skating rink opening up, I'm hoping business will pick up a little for me." He paused. "But you didn't come here just to tell me about a murder attempt."

"Not exactly," said Jimmy. "It seems the man who tried to kill Miss Leighton had a pair of specially modified Rollerblades."

Cohen looked interested. "You don't say."

His voice was steady, but Lois noticed something in his expression. A wariness, she thought. A guardedness.

"I was just checking," she said, "to see if anyone had been here in the last week or two, requesting any modifications to their skates."

The shop owner's brow furrowed. "Modifications? Of what kind?"

"Some sort of accelerators," Lois replied. "Almost like rockets."

A bead of sweat was forming just below Cohen's hairline. This time Lois didn't believe him in the least when he stroked his mustache and shook his head.

"No. I, ah . . . I can't say anyone's been in here asking for anything like that." There seemed to be a tremor in his voice.

Lois paused long enough to let him squirm. "That's funny. If I were looking for someone who could install some tiny jet packs in my Rollerblades, you're the first person I'd think of."

Cohen swallowed. "I—I'm flattered, but . . . no, I didn't do anything like that for anyone."

Lois leaned forward across the sales counter. "I find that difficult to believe, Mr. Cohen."

Suddenly the shop lit up, as Jimmy took a flash shot of the man standing behind his counter. Cohen glared at him, half blinded by the sudden flash.

"I don't want any pictures taken," he insisted.

"Mr. Cohen's right," Lois said, glancing over her shoulder at Jimmy. "He's a decent, honest, hard-working man. And in his heart of hearts, he wants to do the right thing."

She turned to the shop owner and smiled. "Are you *sure* no one has been in here, asking for specially customized skates?"

Cohen cleared his throat. "I guess I'm not a very good liar," he said quietly.

"Not very," Jimmy agreed.

The shop owner frowned and looked at his counter. "A young man was in here a few weeks ago. He had some very small propulsion units that he wanted installed into the heels of his skates. He seemed secretive. And he wanted to pay me in cash."

"So you did the job?" Lois asked.

Cohen looked up and shook his head from side to side. "No. I swear it. It seemed shady, somehow. I told him I didn't have the expertise."

"But you didn't report it to the police," Jimmy noted.

"No," said Cohen, his voice taut. "I didn't. If I had, I wouldn't be here talking to you now—he was that kind of guy. Besides, I didn't know what he wanted to do with the skates. I didn't think he was going to try to kill Janna Leighton."

The man was agitated. Obviously, he wasn't cut

out for dealing with thugs. His greatest crime was that he'd been too scared to say anything.

Lois placed a hand on the shop owner's. "It's all right," she told him. "I know you're not a crook. But it would be a great help to me if you could remember that person's name, or any other information you might have about him."

Cohen considered for a moment. Then he shook his head sadly. "He told me his name, but I don't remember it. At least, I—"

Suddenly his eyes brightened. Turning, he walked over to a desk in the back of the shop and pulled open the top drawer. A moment later he produced a yellow paper.

"What's that?" asked Jimmy.

"A blank work order," Cohen told him. "The guy made me write down a telephone number—and a name. In case I changed my mind, he said."

And Cohen kept the paper. Apparently, thought Lois, he hadn't turned down the job as quickly as he had indicated.

"May I see that?" she asked.

Cohen handed the work order to her. Lois read the name and number and jotted them down on a slip of paper. Then she slipped the paper into her purse. "Thank you for your help, Mr. Cohen."

The man nodded. "You're welcome, Ms. Lane."

With Jimmy a step behind her, Lois turned and hurried out of the shop. As they headed for her car, she opened her purse again, took out her cellular phone, and hurriedly dialed the phone number from the work order.

After three rings, a prim female voice answered. "Good afternoon. Metropolis Suites, front desk."

A hotel? Silently Lois cursed her luck.

"Is there a Mr. Brown staying there?" she asked.

"Just a moment, please," the desk clerk said. There was a loud click on the line as she put Lois on hold.

"Any luck?" Jimmy asked when Lois stopped outside her car.

Lois shook her head. Covering the mouthpiece with her hand, she said, "I think we just hit a dead end."

A moment later the desk clerk came back on the line. "I'm sorry to keep you waiting, ma'am, but there's no Mr. Brown among our guests."

"I see," Lois sighed. "Well, thank you for trying."

Jimmy frowned. "Back to square one?"

Lois nodded. "Unfortunately."

9

THE SOFT GLOW OF CANDLELIGHT lit the spacious dining room in Janna Leighton's twenty-fifth-floor apartment. Clark barely noticed the servants as they whisked away the dessert bowls.

After all, he was much more intrigued by Janna herself. The woman had just escaped death a few hours earlier yet she showed no sign of fear or trepidation. She was a sturdier soul than he had given her credit for.

Behind Janna, sunset gave way to night, and Clark could see the glittering lights of downtown Metropolis. It reminded him that he would have to go soon.

After all, he'd done his work for today. And he had things to do—people to see.

"Thanks for dinner," Clark said, folding his napkin and placing it on the table to one side of his plate.

"Thank the chef," Janna told him. "You know, you surprised me today, Mr. Kent."

"Really?" Clark said, tilting his head. "In what way?"

His hostess smiled. "You're a much better skater than you let on."

Clark shrugged. "Actually, I skated a lot while I was growing up in Smallville. I just hadn't done it since I moved to the big city."

"Of course," she said. "You've been too busy running around after news stories." Turning to one of her servants, she said, "Would you bring me the paper, please, Evelyn?"

The servant paused, her hands full of silverware. "The *Planet*, the *News* or the *Star*, Ms. Leighton?"

The heiress glanced playfully at Clark. "In deference to our guest, the *Planet*. I'm sure Mr. Kent is curious as to how his paper played my near-assassination."

"As you wish," Evelyn said, and left to follow Janna's instructions.

The heiress pushed her chair away from the table and stood up. Walking over to Clark, she indicated with a subtle wave of her hand the sliding glass door that led out on to her balcony.

"You know," he said, "I've really got to go . . . "

"Not just yet," Janna told him.

Giving in, at least for now, Clark stood up and followed her to the door. As Janna unlocked it, the servant arrived with the evening edition of the *Planet.*

Clark paused to accept it and scanned the headline on his way out. Then, as the night breeze ruffled the paper, he took in the story below it at superspeed.

It was Lois's report of the shooting incident at the roller rink this morning. It included a Jimmy Olsen photograph of Danny Grove, tied up beneath the bleachers.

"May I?" asked Janna.

"Of course," he said, handing her the paper.

Leaning against the railing, she read the story— albeit not as quickly as he had. In the meantime, he looked down at the street twenty-five stories below. With his X-ray vision, he could identify each of the half dozen plainclothes cops stationed around the building by the guns in their ankle holsters.

After all, Janna was a target of killers. She needed protection here as much as anywhere else.

"Interesting," she said.

Clark turned to her. "What is?"

Janna smiled appreciatively. "According to this, Superman may have had something to do with my rescue. At least that's what the police are saying. It seems the wheels on the assassin's skates were fused together—and the heat of his propulsion units couldn't have caused that. But someone with heat vision ... "

"It'd be reassuring if he *was* looking out for you," Clark told her.

"That it would," she agreed. "And look at this.

Your friend Lois Lane seems to have discovered what happened in the Cossack Tea Room—despite police efforts to cover it up. And she speculates about other incidents as well."

Janna eyed him.

"Don't look at me," said Clark. "I haven't told her a thing."

"Then she's an extremely perceptive woman," the heiress concluded.

"You don't know the half of it," he replied.

Janna turned to the paper again. "She speculates that these attempts on my life might not be random, but rather an organized conspiracy to eliminate me." She grunted. "A *very* perceptive woman."

Placing the newspaper on a wrought iron table, the heiress took a deep breath of night air and smiled at her companion. Not knowing what else to do, he smiled back.

"So tell me," Janna said. "Do you feel left out? Do you wish you were pounding the pavement alongside your partner?"

Clark looked out at the night sky and the Metropolis skyline as his mind filled with images of Lois. He felt a great longing to be with her—if only to say hello.

But he knew that wouldn't work. Not in the mood Lois was in.

Or would it?

"Clark?" the heiress prodded.

"Huh? Oh, sure," he said finally, in answer to her question. "I miss it a lot. But I've made a commitment here, and I'm not about to drop it at this stage of the game."

He glanced down at his wristwatch and saw that it was getting late. And if he was going to carry out his newfound plan . . .

"Tomorrow's another big day for you," he told Janna. "And for me, too, if today was any indication. I think I'd better go."

She smiled and nodded. "Okay. But do me one favor."

"What's that?" Clark asked.

"Loosen up a bit. You seem so nervous sometimes."

"Nervous? Really?" Clark adjusted his glasses. "Like when?"

"Like just a few seconds ago," Janna replied. "You looked like you were considering jumping right off the balcony. I hope you don't think you're Superman or something."

Clark chuckled. "Never."

As soon as he left Janna's apartment, Clark found an alleyway and slipped into it. A few moments later, he emerged as a blue-and-red blur and took off into the night sky.

Lois's apartment was a mile away, but it only took a few seconds for Superman to cover that distance. As he arrived, he peered in the window.

The lights were off. No one was home. And the window itself was locked, so there was no way he could even leave a message.

What's more, he didn't have the option of sticking around. It wouldn't be a good idea for anyone to see the Man of Steel hovering by the window of Lois Lane's apartment.

Disappointed, Superman headed for Clark Kent's place on Clinton Street. Unfortunately it was going to be another lonely evening, he told himself.

10

As Lois **drove past** Metropolis Stadium early the next morning, her stomach was still groaning. That's what she got for eating Chinese-Mexican food at Jimmy's favorite restaurant late the night before.

Her partner, on the other hand, was a happy fellow. "Man," said Jimmy. "I can still taste those burritos in black bean sauce."

"So can I," Lois told him. "That's the problem."

By now she was used to the sight of the media horde that attended each of Janna's publicity stunts. This time, it was the opening of the Hob's Bay Marina, a brand new, state-of-the-art facility on a stretch of riverside property that had months ago been nothing but weeds.

To mark the event, there would be a sailboat

race. Unfortunately, after the assassination attempt of the day before, there were none of the crowds Janna had no doubt hoped to see. But then, most people didn't want to attend an event where someone might be trying to kill someone else.

On the other hand, there was a considerable police presence. Uniformed officers abounded, and the reporter was sure there were undercover cops here as well.

Lois and Jimmy made their way to the press area, where Janna had already begun fielding questions from behind a podium festooned with microphones. Behind her stood the usual group of sports stars and media personalities, dressed in brightly colored sailing togs—although this time there were some new faces.

"Ms. Leighton," said Lyle Thomas, a reporter for WGBS, "I think it's safe to say that few of the people who live in this section of Metropolis ever expected to enjoy a sailboat ride in their lives. Yet here you are, opening a marina in their backyard. How do you expect them to take advantage of it if they've never sailed?"

Janna smiled as she leaned close to the array of microphones. "A good question, Mr. Thomas—and one we've already addressed. There will be free sailing lessons every Saturday and Sunday for anyone who wants them. All they have to do is sign up.

"As I've said before," she went on, "this is my way of giving back to the city of Metropolis. I don't expect the marina or any of the other facilities I'm donating to Metropolis to turn a profit.

Leighton Industries is picking up the tab as a matter of community relations."

Another reporter shot her hand into the air. It was Linda Gibbs, of the *Eagle*.

"Ms. Leighton, I understand that several of the celebrities slated to participate in today's race have dropped out . . . because of yesterday's unfortunate incident at the skating rink. What are your feelings on that?"

Lois could tell by Janna's expression that this wasn't her favorite question. Nonetheless, she answered it.

"That's right, Linda, we have had a few people pull out—but I can assure you that it was not because of what happened at the skating rink yesterday. Besides, I have found other stars who were more than willing to participate in the event today." With a gesture, she indicated a couple of tall, slim men standing directly behind her. "More specifically, Tim Adams and Fenton Burns of the Metropolis Generals."

The pair stepped forward with a wave. Then they stepped back again.

Despite the grace with which Janna had handled the question, Lois could tell the heiress was uncomfortable with this line of discussion. Wanting to press the point, she asked a follow-up question before Janna could acknowledge any of the other reporters.

"But aren't you creating a dangerous situation here? Where innocent people might get hurt if something else happens?"

"Attagirl," whispered Jimmy, who raised his camera to take a picture at the same time.

Janna looked at the reporter, unflustered. "If there are risks," she said, "then I and all the other participants are well aware of them. What's more, we accept them. These events are all for a good cause—to benefit the citizens of Metropolis. The television cameras are waiting, and we are not going to be intimidated."

Lois was about to pose another question, but Janna took command and cut her off.

"That's all the time we have for this," she said. "We have a sailboat race to get started. Thank you all very much for coming here today, and I hope— we *all* hope—that you enjoy yourselves."

With that, Janna and her celebrity teams started toward the docks to board their respective sailboats. Along with the other reporters, Lois and Jimmy followed them.

They walked down to the water's edge and took up a position right near one of the WGBS cameramen. This gave them a good view of the course, which was marked by three red buoys, one for each leg of the race.

Lois wasn't the least bit surprised to see that Clark was on Janna's team. Like the heiress and Will Paulson of the Monarchs, he was wearing a red windbreaker.

Jimmy shook his head and chuckled. "Clark grew up in the Midwest. What does he know about sailing?"

"Absolutely nothing," Lois replied.

On the other hand, he could probably paddle the boat from here to Maine and still get back in time to win the race. But of course, she didn't say that, not even to Jimmy.

A small craft—the committee boat—was anchored near the buoys that marked the finish line of the triangular racecourse. Mayor Berkowitz and Police Commissioner Henderson were on board. Berkowitz raised a helium horn to signal the start of the race.

As the sound of the horn—something like the cry of a wounded whale—echoed across the bay, the irregular line of sailboats, their triangular sails bellied out, darted past the buoy markers.

The race was on.

11

SITTING ON THE PORT SIDE of Janna's boat with the wind at his back, Clark couldn't quite enjoy the sensation of flying across the water. His main reason for being here—at least from Superman's point of view—was to keep watch over the heiress, and that's what he intended to do.

Of course, he had never done much sailing, so he had to pay at least some attention to Janna's commands. But he was also on the lookout for any potential danger. In the last two days alone, there had been three attempts on Janna's life, and he knew there would probably be more.

Before the race, Clark had scanned all the other contestants and their sailboats with his X-ray vision. An unnecessary precaution, as it turned out. Everyone was exactly what he or she seemed to be.

Then again, an attack—if there was one—probably wouldn't come from one of the racers. There were plenty of other craft out on the bay this morning, including a wide variety of recreational motorboats and even some large commercial vessels, heading to and from Metropolis's busy docks.

Of course, any of these boats could cross the regatta's course, as long as they didn't interfere with the race. Therefore, any one of them could present a danger to Janna.

Two helicopters hovered overhead with TV news markings. Clark couldn't rule out a threat from that quarter, either. And assassins could be lurking onshore as well, just waiting for a clear shot.

But at least for now, everything looked safe. Clark could haul on the lines that trimmed the foresail, and not have to worry too much.

In a short time, they'd reached the first buoy. With flapping sails, they made their way around it, shifting from a port tack to a starboard one.

As the heavy aluminum boom swung around, Clark ducked down low. Even then, it didn't miss his head by much. He knew it couldn't possibly have hurt him, but his head would have dented the boom, and he didn't want either of his crewmates to see that.

Little by little, Janna's boat forged ahead of the others, despite the relative inexperience of her crew. It was clear from her expression that, despite any prospect of danger, she was enjoying herself immensely.

For the next several minutes, Clark and his crewmates occupied themselves with simply sailing the boat. Janna shouted encouragement to him and Will Paulson, complimenting them on the job they were doing.

By the time they were nearing the second buoy, Clark was tempted to relax. Maybe there wasn't going to be an attempt on Janna's life today. Maybe the assassins had finally given up.

No way, said a voice in his head. *Something's coming. It's just a matter of when.*

"Ready about," Janna cried out. They were approaching the second buoy and the last leg of the course.

"Ready," Paulson shouted heartily.

Remaining alert for any trouble, Clark prepared for the turn. When he looked back at their competition, he saw that they were only a couple of boatlengths behind.

"Hard alee," Janna yelled, pushing the tiller away from her.

Paulson released the foresail so they could come about. But just before the boat turned around the buoy, Clark saw what looked like trouble.

Earlier, he had noticed a large motor yacht, but it hadn't exhibited any strange behavior. Now it was plowing toward them through the water at breakneck speed.

Clark tensed, wondering whether the boat would try to ram them. But instead it stopped—so suddenly, in fact, that it was nearly swamped by its own wake.

As Clark watched, the front of the yacht dropped open. A loud hum like a swarm of angry hornets filled the air—and a pack of sleek black jet-skis ripped out of the bowels of the boat into the water.

All of the jet-ski drivers were wearing dark wet suits and goggles. And they were all armed with some kind of high-tech machine guns.

Clark knew he had to act fast. Lowering his glasses, he prepared to give each jet-ski a blast of his heat vision.

But the assassins were more clever than he had anticipated—and more skilled. Before Clark could act, they were in among the other sailboats, using them for cover.

He couldn't use his heat vision without possibly injuring the other racers. Nor could the cops onshore do anything, for the same reason.

Weaving ever closer as they cut through the blue water of the bay, the jet-skis sent up a roar. Glancing at Janna, Clark saw the strain on her face—the beginnings of fear.

But to her credit, she wasn't panicking. Much to the contrary, in fact. She seemed to be wracking her brain for a way out of their predicament.

Suddenly the heiress thrust the tiller away from her, as she'd done before when she wanted to change direction. Coming as quickly as it did, her action swung the boat around. The sails started to shift to a position where they would conceal the crew from the jet-skiers.

As the boom swung toward him, Clark saw his

opportunity. Rather than duck, he kept his head high—where the boom could smack into it. Of course, he jerked his head away at the last second, but no observer would be able to tell that.

Then, faking a pained outcry, Clark flipped over the railing. He took a deep breath as he hit the water. Using his superhearing, he heard both Janna and Paulson call out to him, but he had no intention of reassuring them—at least not yet.

As quickly as he could, he stripped off his clothes and stowed them in a small pouch in his cape. Then he looked up at the surface.

Superman could see the bottom of the hull of Janna's sailboat as it swung about. And he could see the zigzag wakes of the approaching jet-skis. At best, Janna had only bought herself a few more seconds.

There was no time to lose. Kicking hard, Superman shot up out of the water—right into the path of the assassins.

When they saw the Man of Steel, the killers hesitated for a moment, out of surprise. Then they turned their weapons on him and opened fire.

The air exploded with the sound of gunfire, but the bullets bounced harmlessly off Superman's chest and sizzled into the water. Then, moving much faster than the jet-skis, Superman darted from one to another, pausing just long enough to disarm the assassins and punch a hole in each jet engine.

Five in all, he counted. But there had been six . .
.

Whirling, he saw that one of the jet-skis had taken a roundabout route toward Janna's boat. And right now its driver was closing in on his target, trying to steady his aim as he bobbled on the choppy water.

Superman didn't give him a chance. Instead, he sucked in a deep breath and directed a mighty stream at the assassin's back.

Instantly the gunman went flying over the front of his jet-ski and hit the water—hard. Still roaring, the jet-ski bounced up out of the water and ran in a wide circle around Janna's boat.

However, its driver—unconscious now—was in danger of drowning. Without hesitation, Superman grabbed him just before he went under. Then, flying fast, he carried the unconscious man over to the committee boat and deposited him in front of Commissioner Henderson.

"Nice work," the commissioner said.

Superman didn't stick around to acknowledge the compliment. Satisfied that the police could round up the other attackers, he streaked off into the sky.

As soon as he was out of sight, however, Superman angled down and dove into the water. Swimming as fast as he could, he made his way back toward Janna's sailboat until he could see it from below.

His X-ray vision showed him that the heiress and Will Paulson were scanning the surface of the water for him. Janna looked more afraid for Clark than she had been for herself.

Eliminating all evidence that he was Superman, he changed back into his sailing togs. Then, with one last, strong stroke, he popped up to the surface just behind Janna's boat.

"Hey!" he cried. "Over here!"

Janna turned and caught a glimpse of him over her stern. "Oh my gosh! *Clark!*"

Latching on to the boat, Clark raised his right hand and waved weakly to her. While Janna held the tiller to keep the boat pointed into the wind, Paulson did his best to haul Clark back on board. With an effort on his part, he succeeded.

"Wha-what happened?" Clark said. He shook his head as though dazed.

"The boom caught you on the head," Paulson told him. "You're gonna have one heck of an egg there."

Clark gingerly touched the side of his head. He winced and cried out softly as though he had hit a tender spot.

"Wow," he said. "That smarts."

He glanced at the other sailors, then at the disabled jet-skis and the police boat that had begun to move among them. Also, he caught a glimpse of a couple of Coast Guard ships converging on the motor yacht that had carried the assassins in its hold.

Finally he turned to Janna and said soberly, "Another close call."

She frowned and looked away from him, for the first time showing the stress of the attempts on her life. "Come on," she said. "Let's take her back to the dock. And look lively about it. I don't want those creeps to think they've shut us down."

* * *

From the shoreline, Lois was watching through binoculars as Will Paulson helped Clark out of the water. She shook her head.

Clark was doing a good job of faking it, but she knew he'd never been in danger. He'd only ducked out of the way so he could appear as Superman.

"Nice," she muttered.

"What's that?" Jimmy asked, looking at her quizzically.

Lois shook her head. "Nothing." She kept the binoculars pressed to her eyes as Jimmy snapped off shot after shot of the police fishing the assassins out of the water.

"Well," he said matter-of-factly, "it doesn't look like you're going to get the scoop on this one."

"Oh, I wouldn't be so sure," Lois replied. Lowering the binoculars, she turned to him. "Come on. Let's get going."

He glanced at her. "Where to now?"

"Think about it. Where would a bunch of gunmen get a fleet of jet-skis? And a customized motor yacht?"

Jimmy considered for a moment, then shrugged and said, "A boatyard, I guess."

"Exactly," Lois told him. "And there aren't all *that* many boatyards in and around Metropolis. Let's go around and ask a few questions."

Jimmy looked hesitant. "You know, I really ought to get back to the *Planet* and develop these pictures. Otherwise they won't get into the evening edition."

He was right about that. But at the same time, she didn't want to give the trail time to get cold.

"Okay," Lois said. "Tell you what. I'll check out a couple of places on my own, and we'll hook up later."

Jimmy nodded. "It's a deal."

He hefted his equipment and turned to leave, but something stopped him. He glanced at Lois over his shoulder.

"You'll be careful, right?"

She managed a sardonic smile. "Aren't I always?"

Jimmy chuckled. "That's exactly what I was afraid of."

As he walked away in search of a taxi, Lois was already plumbing her memory for the location of the nearest boatyard. If memory served, there was one in New Troy . . .

Later that day, the bearded man stood in front of the window of his hotel suite, high above Metropolis. The sky was a startling blue.

The man's hands were clenched into fists. "Superman," he breathed, his voice tinged with a foreign accent.

Closing his eyes, he took a deep breath to control his rising anger. Then, turning slowly, he scanned the group of men standing in the room a short distance behind him.

"Clearly," the bearded man said, "the costumed one has realized what we are doing. We have to take him into account now."

His compatriots nodded. There was a short chorus of agreement.

The bearded man nailed each of them with a cold stare. "Five attempts. First, the one at the Leighton woman's office. Then the one at the restaurant. The sniper at the sports arena makes three, the roller rink four—and the jet-ski effort five.

"All of them failed. All ended in futility. And now that this Superman is involved, it will be even more difficult." The bearded man grunted. "I will no longer tolerate excuses. You understand?"

He could feel his face flushing with shame and embarrassment, anger and frustration. This was not the way he had planned it. It was taking too long. They were beginning to look like fools.

"From now on," he said, in a barely controlled voice, "we will do whatever is necessary, Superman or no Superman. We will succeed, no matter the cost."

The others voiced their agreement. They were with him. He had but to say the word, and they would lay down their lives for him.

He gave a thin-lipped smile. Then he turned to the window again and looked out at the sky. Clasping his hands together behind his back, he wrung them so tightly he could feel his knuckles turn white.

"Wherever you are right now, Janna Leighton . . . whatever you are doing," he said, "I promise you—you will not live to enjoy the fruits of your labors."

12

By 11:00 a.m., Lois had pulled her car into the parking lot at the New Troy Marina. Snooping around, she found several boats in various stages of reconstruction and repair, but not a whole lot else.

The workers in the yard didn't even question her as she walked around. It wasn't exactly the kind of atmosphere one associated with secrecy or criminal dealings.

The manager of the marina was a jolly old fellow who could have been driving a sleigh on Christmas Eve. Of course, he'd heard about the assassination attempt at Hob's Bay via the radio, and he was aghast—genuinely, Lois decided. Following her instincts, she gave New Troy a clean bill of health and moved on.

Her next stop was Harbor Lights Boatyard. As she drove up to the entrance, it occurred to her that the place had been owned by Howard Marsten, before he'd sold everything and moved to Paris. Under his direction, the boatyard had become the leading boatbuilder and renovator in the Metropolis area.

The most prosperous, too. Unfortunately, it didn't look that way now.

The yard itself, once known for its opulence and even glamor, was a weed-choked field; Lois could see that from the outside. What's more, there were fewer boats here than at New Troy. Apparently the place had fallen on hard times after Marsten's departure.

Something about it gave her the creeps. Following her instincts, she drove past the yard and parked in a lot across the street.

Having decided not to enter by the "front door," Lois made her way to the chain link fence surrounding the boatyard. The top of the fence was lined with razor wire, so scaling it would be impossible.

She walked the perimeter until she found a narrow gap in the fence through which she could squeeze. If there were guard dogs or other security measures, she didn't see any evidence of them.

Once inside, she wandered between row after row of boats set upright in wooden cradles. Mixed in with a few expensive-looking pleasure craft were a great many lobster and fishing boats.

Harbor Lights had always catered exclusively to

the very rich. That it no longer did so was further evidence of its decline.

Lois wasn't sure what she was looking for, but she kept moving about, zigzagging between the boats. Eventually she came to a huge barn. She could make out a long, sloping ramp that ran from the double doors to the water's edge.

She moved closer to the barn. A sign above the side door read BOAT CUSTOMIZING AND PAINTING. So that's what the barn was for, she mused.

The side door was open. Through it she could see lights on inside. She heard voices and the sounds of people moving about. Unfortunately she couldn't hear what they were saying.

But a window had been left open. Using the boats and a cluster of empty oil drums for cover, she snuck up to it. Ever so slowly, she rose up on tiptoe and peered over the edge of the windowsill.

There were three men inside the dimly lit barn. Lois didn't recognize any of them. One was overweight, wearing a shirt and tie, and had to be either the new owner or his manager. He was seated at a desk, surrounded by a mess of papers and old sailing magazines.

In the center of the mess stood a computer terminal. The screen threw the overweight man's face into stark relief.

The two other men, younger than the first and in much better shape, were in T-shirts and overalls. One wore a cloth apron splattered with an assortment of brightly colored paints. All three were drinking coffee and munching doughnuts.

The boss slammed his beefy fist on the desk, almost spilling his coffee. "I don't see how we can get any more jet-skis till the end of next week. Damn! And just as the season is starting, too!"

"How much they gonna cost?" the man in the paint-splattered apron asked. His jaw muscles worked hard on a bite of doughnut.

"More than the six we lost yesterday," the boss said. He shook his head. "Figures the price would go up. You can't win for losing."

"Hey," said the third man, "you knew you weren't gonna get 'em back. Ain't that why you had us file the serial numbers off? So's the police couldn't trace 'em back here?"

"Yeah," muttered the overweight man, "don't rub it in. Too bad I didn't ask those jerks for more money. If I'da known how long I'd be without the mothers . . . "

Lois dropped down below the edge of the window, breathing hard. The men had to be talking about the jet-skis the assassins had used at Hob's Bay. Having given up their supply, they were having a hard time getting more on short notice.

And if they'd supplied the gunmen with the jet-skis, they'd probably also modified the motor yacht. This was more than she'd dreamed she would find when she snuck into the yard.

But right now, she was pressing her luck. Any second, one of the men might wander outside and see her lurking around.

Of course, Lois was tempted to investigate a bit more. It would be doubly satisfying to find some hard evidence connecting these men to the murder attempt. A printout from the company computer, for instance.

But right now, it was too much of a risk. Besides, she already had enough information to get the police out here to investigate.

Lois was just turning to leave when she heard a shuffling sound on the dry ground behind her. She broke into a run but had taken no more than two or three steps when she felt someone grab her by the shoulder.

A deep voice boomed out, "What are you doin' here?"

Turning, she saw a hulking bear of a man— probably another worker here. Judging from his expression, she wasn't going to be able to talk her way out of this one.

There was only one other option.

Balancing on one foot, Lois whirled and clipped the man across the jaw with the heel of her shoe. As he staggered, she stepped forward and drove her fist straight into his solar plexus, nearly breaking her hand in the process.

The man gasped and stumbled backward a few steps. Lois didn't wait to see if he was going to fall. She just ducked her head and ran for all she was worth.

She heard someone shout at her, "Hey, you! Stop right there!"

Lois dared to look back. The two men in overalls had come out of the barn and caught sight of her. Both of them were aiming guns in her direction!

The man who had tried to stop her was still doubled over. But that wouldn't be the case for long, she told herself. And anyway, those two gunmen didn't need any help.

Darting between two rows of boats, Lois heard a gun go off. It was followed by a loud *ping* that sounded close to her head—much *too* close. The bullet had ricocheted off one of the hulls. Keeping her head down, she continued to run as gunfire exploded like thunder in the boatyard.

"Superman, where are you?" she whispered.

But she knew the Man of Steel wasn't going to hear her. She was on her own this time.

It took Lois much longer than she had hoped to find the gap in the chain link fence. Finally she made it outside the boatyard and raced back toward her car. The sound of gunfire had stopped, but she had no idea how close the men were behind her.

Grabbing the remote control from her purse, Lois unlocked the car as she ran. Gasping for breath, she opened the door and practically dove onto the front seat. Her hands shook as she fumbled with the keys.

As Lois cranked the key in the ignition, the car roared to life. She shifted into gear and tromped on the accelerator. A spray of dirt shot out from under the tires.

Glancing in her rearview mirror, she saw a car speed out of the boatyard. After a moment's hesitation, the driver—still wearing his paint-splattered apron—turned his vehicle in her direction and gunned the engine.

Fortunately, Lois's car was faster. Smiling grimly, she sped up and quickly put distance between herself and her pursuers. She was confident that she had enough of a lead on these guys to ditch them.

Gripping the steering wheel tightly with one hand, Lois took out her cellular phone with the other and dialed the main precinct of the Metropolis Police.

The desk sergeant answered briskly. "Downtown."

"Detective Bradley, please," she said. "It's Lois Lane."

She and Bradley knew each other from half a dozen cases. Lois knew she could depend on him.

"Right," the desk sergeant replied. "Hang on, lady. It'll be a minute."

Lois heard a click as he put her on hold. While she waited, she forced herself to take deep, even breaths. She could still see the other car in her mirror.

Suddenly the boatyard men broke off the chase. Slamming on the brakes, they spun around and headed back the way they had come.

"Slam Bradley here," a gruff voice answered at last.

Breathing a sigh of relief, Lois related what had just happened.

"Geez," he said. "Are you all right?"

"I'm fine," she told him. "If you get over there right away, I bet you'll catch all four of them red-handed."

Bradley grunted his assent. "Thanks for the tip, Lois. I owe you one."

He owed her *several*, she thought. But one would do for now.

Joe Dugan, owner of the Harbor Lights Boatyard, was sitting at his cluttered desk, his pudgy fingers racing across the keyboard as he dumped all information concerning jet-ski purchases and sales.

Suddenly, Lenny—his hull-painting specialist—burst into the barn, out of breath.

"The cops," he said. "They're here, Joe!"

Herb and Marco were right behind him. Marco had a black and blue spot along the line of his jaw, where the nosy woman had kicked him. More than likely, Joe thought, she was a cop, too.

Ignoring Lenny's warning, Joe went about his business, eliminating file after file. The painter stuck his face in front of Joe's.

"Didn't ya hear me?" he asked, his voice high-pitched and frantic. "It's the cops!"

"What a surprise," the fat man said sarcastically.

"Well?" asked Herb. "Whaddaya want us to do?"

Joe glanced at him. "I don't want you to do anything," he said as calmly as he could. "It's too late for that. You put the guns back in the safe, right? Now you can sit tight while I—"

Before he could finish his sentence, he caught a glimpse through the side window of a police car with its emergency lights flashing. As it stopped in front of the open doorway, it fishtailed and raised a cloud of dust.

A couple of uniformed policemen and some

kind of detective rushed into the barn, their guns drawn. Joe reminded himself to stay cool.

Keeping his forefinger pressed down on one particular key, he deleted all remaining boatyard records for the last six months. When he was done, he stood up and regarded his visitors.

"What's the problem here?" he asked, feigning indignance.

The detective's eyes narrowed. Clearly he wasn't buying Joe's act.

"We got a report of some gunshots out here a while ago," he said.

"Is that so?" Joe responded. He stood up and walked around the side of his desk. "Well, you see, someone was trying to break in here and steal my stuff, so my security guards took a coupla shots at 'em. I got signs posted all around the place, sayin' there's armed guards on duty. You got a problem with that?"

The detective laughed. "Yeah, as a matter of fact, I do—especially when I've got reason to believe you were mixed up in that jet-ski attack at Hob's Bay."

Joe's mouth went dry. Okay, he told himself, the woman had heard them talking. But it wasn't evidence they could use in court. And he had already dumped the computer files.

"Tell you what," said the detective. "How about you come down to the station and answer a few questions? You shouldn't mind that, being a law-abiding businessman and all—right?"

Joe swallowed. "Am I under arrest?"

The detective smiled. "Do birds fly?"

Scowling, Joe turned to Lenny. "Keep an eye on the place for me."

"I don't think you get it," the detective told him. "You're *all* coming with us. We're going to go down to the station, where we'll have a nice little chat with each of you."

Joe looked at his men. He didn't think Herb would talk, and Marco didn't really know much. But Lenny was out for himself. It'd be just like him to turn state's evidence . . .

"Come on," said the detective, taking him by the arm. "We haven't got all day. And by the way, you have the right to remain silent . . . "

13

"Penny for your thoughts?" Janna said, over the orchestral music lilting in the background.

Clark looked at her. "I think you can guess."

"Lois Lane," she replied flatly, heaping some more fruit and cheese on her plate.

Clark nodded. "Right the first time."

They were moving alongside an overloaded buffet table at the heiress's country club. But as appetizing as the spread of roasted meats, cheeses, fruits, and vegetables looked, Clark wasn't feeling all that hungry. Apparently it showed.

Janna frowned. "You know, Clark, I've got a confession to make."

"What's that?" he asked.

"At first," she said, "I didn't understand what you saw in Lois. I mean, she is a pretty face and all, but those are a dime a dozen. I understand now, though. She's bright, insightful, clever, persistent . . . ."

All those things, Clark agreed silently. *And more.*

He hadn't loved the idea of having lunch here. It was too ostentatious for his taste—as if he were purposely flaunting his association with Janna. But as the heiress had pointed out, both of them had to eat, and this was as good a place as any to soothe their jangled nerves.

And despite her outward calm, her nerves had to be jangled. Once again, she'd come within a hair's breadth of being killed.

He recalled the frenzy of the reporters just a couple of hours ago, as Janna steered her boat back to the dock. In the wake of the ruined races, they had clustered around her, wondering if she would cancel the final charity event on her schedule.

Janna had told them that the event—a softball game—was very definitely still on. "I have a debt to pay," she'd said. "A *huge* debt. On behalf of my father's memory. And I'm not going to let down either the community or the charities that will profit from what I'm doing."

Of course, those behind the assassination attempt would likely try again. But that didn't seem to deter Janna in the least.

"I should tell you something else," the heiress added.

Clark glanced at her as he forked sliced meats and vegetables onto his plate. "I'm listening."

"I've seen the way Lois looks at you," Janna told him. "I take back what I said about her and

Howard Marsten. It was in bad taste. The woman has eyes only for you, I'm afraid."

Clark sighed. "I hope you're right. After what's happened the last few days, I don't know if she'll even speak to me again."

Janna chuckled. "She'll speak to you, all right. Trust me on that."

He grunted. "How do you know?"

His companion patted him gently on the cheek. "I'm a woman, aren't I?"

Lois stared through the one-way mirror at Joe, the boatyard owner. He was sitting alone in the police station's interrogation room, his head cradled in his hands.

Slam Bradley hadn't needed more than half an hour to crack the man's resolve. Or so he'd said.

First he'd told Joe of a case he had recently, where a crook tried to dump all his computer files. Of course, that had only made the police suspect the crook all the more. Then Bradley remarked on how a computer expert could salvage such files even after they'd been erased.

That loosened Joe up a little. That's when Bradley rolled out his big gun—the one about how Lenny and Herb and Marco were sitting in interrogation rooms of their own, each bargaining to save his skin at the expense of his friends.

Apparently, Joe already had suspicions regarding Lenny's ability to keep his mouth shut. He'd taken Bradley's advice and spilled his guts before any of the others could.

"Come on," Lois said, turning to face the detective. "I'm the one who tipped you off. The least you can do is tell me what the creep said."

Bradley, straddling a nearby chair, shrugged a little. "He said he had nothing to do with the attempt on Janna Leighton's life yesterday."

Lois cast him a withering glance. "Don't play games," she said. "I mean *after* he turned stool pigeon."

"Oh." Bradley hesitated.

"One hand washes the other," she reminded him.

After a moment, he nodded. "Okay. But this could be a big deal. I want you to keep it under your hat for a while."

"What's a while?" Lois asked.

"Whatever I say."

Lois laughed. "That's a joke, right?"

"No joke," he told her. His expression underlined the fact. "I mean it. No article in the *Planet* until I give you the go-ahead."

Lois thought it over. Certainly she didn't like the idea of sitting on a story. But if that was the only way to get it, she would put her likes and dislikes aside.

"All right," Lois promised. "I'll keep it out of the paper till you say otherwise."

"Good," said Bradley. "Then here it is. It seems this guy Joe hasn't been doing too well with the boatyard. It's been going downhill ever since he bought it from Howard Marsten."

Lois nodded. "Nothing I didn't know from looking at the place."

The detective ignored her and went on. "He was losing money, afraid that the bank would foreclose on him. Maybe he talks to a couple of people, and they talk to a couple of other people. Anyway, a guy walks into Joe's office one day. He says his name is Brown—"

"Brown?" Lois asked.

Bradley nodded. "Yeah. You know something about that?"

She told him about her encounter with the skate shop owner. "He said the guy who approached him used the name Brown."

"Then it's probably not a coincidence," the detective concluded, making a note. "According to our pal Joe, this Brown fella started out wanting to buy some jet-skis. Then, little by little, he enticed Joe into something bigger."

"Into customizing a motor yacht," Lois guessed, "so it could hold a bunch of jet-skiers with guns."

"Exactly," said Bradley, a little surprised. "Fortunately for us, Mr. Brown has a big mouth. Maybe he figured he had Joe in his pocket— maybe he meant to shut him up permanently later on. In any case, he tells Joe he's from Quarac. So Joe asks this Brown guy if he's with the Quaraci government—which would be bad enough, in my opinion. Brown says no, he's with some kind of terrorist group."

Lois looked at him. "Terrorists? From the Middle East? But why would they be so hot and heavy to kill Janna Leighton? What could she have done to them?"

"I don't know," the detective replied. "And apparently neither does Joe. Maybe it's because she's become a symbol of hope around here. Or maybe they just don't like blondes. The point is, they want her dead."

The reporter mulled over what she had just learned. Was Clark being secretive because he didn't want people to know about the terrorist angle? Because he figured it would cause a panic in Metropolis?

That was a possibility. But certainly he knew he could trust *her*. It frustrated her to believe otherwise.

"Okay," she said, dragging her attention back to the case. "So they want to kill her. But why try to do it in such public places? Why not just have her quietly assassinated?"

Bradley leaned back in his chair. "I suppose that would be easier for them, if all they were interested in was the result. But a quiet assassination wouldn't make a big enough point for their cause, would it?"

Lois nodded. That made sense. Terrorists all wanted to send messages of some kind. The louder, the better.

"And Janna's too much of an egotist to back down," Lois observed. "She'd rather risk her life and the lives of her friends than give in to these terrorists."

The detective looked at her. "You know, as a cop, I hate the idea that people like Leighton are putting themselves in the line of fire. It makes my job hell. But the private citizen in me likes what she's doing. She's standing up to these jerks, telling them that they can't come to Metropolis and make us do whatever they want. That takes guts."

Lois was reluctant to admit it, but Bradley had a point. Janna *did* have guts. She wasn't just a spoiled little rich girl throwing her daddy's money around.

"Did Joe tell you anything else?" she asked. "Anything that would give you a line on the terrorist leadership?"

"Not really," the detective answered. "Brown's nowhere to be found. So all we've got is a bunch of would-be killers who won't talk—not about who they work for or where they might strike next, or anything."

Lois eyed him. "You think they'll take another stab at her during tonight's softball game?"

"Hard to say," Bradley remarked. "On the one hand, it's the last chance for them to make a big public statement. But on the other, the place will be swarming with cops. And now it looks like Superman's got an interest in this thing, too. They might not want to mess around with the Man of Steel, if you know what I mean."

It was true. The Superman factor might be enough to scare the killers off. But somehow Lois doubted it.

"Your best guess?" she inquired.

"Best guess?" he echoed. "The creeps try to get to Leighton on the softball field. They don't call 'em fanatics for nothing."

14

IT WAS A BEAUTIFUL SPRING EVENING. The sun had already set, and huge banks of high-powered lights shone down on the brand-new, manicured softball field less than a block from Metropolis Stadium.

Gazing at such a tableau from afar, one would never guess how much tension was in the air. Yet Lois felt it from her place in the newly-fashioned stands, not far from the third baseline. And judging from his expression, so did Jimmy.

It wasn't at all like that first night, when Janna's plan had seemed so bright and promising, and crowds of onlookers and reporters had gathered in the shadow of the stadium to hear her words of hope. Now the only spectators were a large contingent of Leighton Industries employees, out to show their support for the chairman of their board. All the neighborhood people had ended up staying home.

Of course there were more reporters than ever. If there was another attempt on the heiress's life, every newspaper and TV station from Metropolis to San Francisco wanted their people on hand to cover it. It was a little ghoulish, Lois reflected, but that was a reality of the news game.

There were plenty of cops as well, both uniformed and otherwise, she imagined. And a new wrinkle—a sprinkling of men and women with FBI windbreakers.

A handful of brave vendors hawked hot dogs and Soder Cola. But if one looked closely, it was obvious that even they were on the lookout for anything out of the ordinary.

As before, WGBS had deployed its full complement of cameramen, soundmen, directors, producers, and on-camera talent. After all, the station had paid a lot of money to cover Janna's charity events. And now that there was an element of danger to them, television ratings were likely to go through the roof.

The dark bulk of the WGBS blimp hovered overhead. The view from the blimp was visible on the huge Jumbo-Tron screen that had been erected in center field.

Turning to Jimmy, Lois asked, "Are you sure you want to be here?"

Her partner smiled at her. "Are you?"

"Not really," she told him.

"Neither am I," he said. "I mean, I keep checking

the bottom of my seat for bombs. But I don't think I'm scared enough to leave. Besides . . . "

"Yes?"

"One way or the other, there's going to be a story here tonight. Someone's got to cover it for the *Planet*, right?"

Lois smiled at him. Jimmy was the quintessential go-getter, the newshound on the trail of a story. But then, it took one to know one.

Jimmy hailed a vendor. "Hey," he yelled, "over here!"

The vendor came over and set down his metal case full of hot dogs. He was a burly man, with graying hair and glasses.

"How many?" he asked, looking up.

Jimmy turned to Lois. "Want one?"

She shook her head. She was too nervous to eat, too full of adrenaline.

"One," Jimmy told the man.

"One it is." With a flourish, he took a set of tongs and fished out a hot dog from the hot water within. Then he took out a roll and laid the hot dog inside. "Mustard?"

Jimmy nodded. A moment later he received the hot dog and a mustard packet in the bargain.

Jimmy paid the vendor, and the man proceeded to his next customer. As Jimmy bit into the hot dog, Lois was reminded of their experience at the Mexican-Chinese restaurant. Apparently her friend Jimmy could eat anything, anytime.

Suddenly a loud trumpet fanfare blasted over the speakers lining the field. One by one, the various members of the celebrity teams were introduced.

The players trotted out of the dugouts and lined up along the baselines. They were clad in red or blue softball outfits, depending on which team they belonged to.

Once again, Lois noticed that some of Janna's stars had deserted her, particularly the WLEX personalities and some of the Meteors. And again, she had found replacements for them, this time drawing from the Metropolis hockey team.

Clark was in uniform, too, one of the last to reach the dugout. Lois noticed how he scanned the field—no doubt using his X-ray vision to see things no one else could.

It reassured her that he apparently hadn't found anything to be alarmed about—at least not yet. Then again, the evening was still young.

She also felt a little better about Clark's sudden penchant for secrecy, though not as much as she would have liked. He must have known all along about the threat to Janna. What started out as a legitimate story idea must have become an excuse to remain on hand and protect her as Superman, when and if the need arose.

But why not tell Lois? Why not share his secret with the woman he claimed to love? That question still stuck in Lois's craw.

Before she knew it, the national anthem was piped in. Mayor Berkowitz threw out the first ball, and the game began.

Settling in to watch, Lois noticed that Clark

wasn't playing. Instead, he was coaching third base for the blue team—maybe because of his "injury" during the sailboat race the day before.

The first batter struck out, and the second one grounded out to shortstop. But the third batter—Steve Lombard of WGBS—hit a double into right field. When the right fielder misplayed it, he moved on to third, where Clark signaled to hold him up.

The crowd stood and cheered. But Lois's gaze was drawn to Clark. As if aware of the scrutiny, he turned and looked back at her.

Their eyes met. He raised his hand and waved, ever so slightly. Smiling, she waved back.

Without really saying anything, they'd spoken volumes. Clark knew that Lois knew about the terrorists—she could see it in his expression. And Lois was sure that Clark knew how hard she was trying to understand him.

Things weren't all patched up yet, but it was a start.

Clark returned his attention to the game. Or at least he appeared to. In fact, he would be maintaining his terrorist watch.

There was still a good chance there would be another attempt on Janna Leighton's life tonight. But no one knew where it would come from, or when it would take place.

The bearded man frowned as he gazed at the wide-screen television he'd requested from room service. The sole source of light in the room, it cast a cold blue glow over everything.

Over the furnishings, over the walls, even over his men, who were as intent on the screen as he was. The bearded man himself stood at the opposite end of the room, by the large picture window that looked over Metropolis.

"Look," said Jamal, his passport and customs expert. "It is *she*."

Jamal was correct. The screen had filled with a close-up of Janna Leighton, who was approaching home plate with a bat in her hands. As she crouched, the opposing pitcher went into his windup.

The bearded man knew much about baseball. After all, he had been in this country for nearly a year. One could not reside in the United States without learning *something* about "the national pastime."

He even had a favorite team—the Gotham Knights. He liked them mainly because they had beaten the Monarchs in the play-offs last year. The Monarchs, after all, had been the darlings of Alexander Leighton. Anything that made Alexander Leighton unhappy was a good thing in the bearded man's book.

Alexander Leighton . . . the man who had ruined Quarac. The man whose chemical plants lay like sores across the Quaraci landscape.

In this country, Leighton could not have built such plants. In the United States, there were stringent safety and environmental standards. But not so in Quarac.

Knowing this, Leighton had established a relationship with the corrupt Quaraci government. He found cheap labor in the Quaraci population, people who were willing to work for a few dollars a day, with no thought as to the hazards their work might entail.

Fourteen months earlier, an explosion in one of Leighton's Quaraci factories had released a cloud of toxic gas, killing a great many people.

One of them was the bearded man's son. His nineteen-year-old son. His *only* son.

Leighton never made reparations to the families of the victims. It seemed it was not in his contract with the Quaraci government. And if he was not obliged to spend money, he invariably chose not to.

Fortunately, the bearded man was a high-ranking operative in a terrorist cell. There were avenues open to him, ways of avenging himself against Alexander Leighton. But Leighton had died before the bearded man could exact retribution from the devil for his crimes.

At first, the bearded man had been shocked by the news of Leighton's death. Then he heard the name Janna Leighton and learned of her intention to take over for her father, and he knew he still had a goal worth achieving.

If he could not destroy the father, he would destroy the daughter—the one person Alexander Leighton had most loved in the world. After all, was she not a parasite? Was she not living off the profits soaked in Quaraci blood? In his *son's* blood?

The bearded man had vowed to destroy Janna Leighton, no matter how long it took to set up an organization here in the United States. And in the process, he would also destroy her attempt to cleanse her father's name.

He had not wavered in that purpose. And he would not waver now, Superman or no Superman.

Justice would be done.

Finally, he had arranged something that even Superman would not be able to stop. Soon his work in Metropolis would be over.

Feeling a hand on his shoulder, the bearded man turned. It was Hakeem, his weapons expert.

Hakeem smiled, stretching out the scar that ran from his chin to his brow. "We will not fail you tonight, Abu. We are resolved to sacrifice everything—even our lives—in the name of the Quaraci people and what they have suffered at the hands of Alexander Leighton."

Abu nodded. "That is good to hear."

Hakeem reached into his pocket and withdrew a long, serrated dagger. Raising the blade to eye level, he flicked the edge with his thumb and drew a dark drop of blood. It symbolized his commitment to their goal.

Abu turned back to the screen, where Janna Leighton's team was now taking the field. "Yes," he said, "that is *very* good."

15

LOIS WAS BEGINNING TO WONDER if she hadn't been mistaken after all. It was the bottom of the sixth inning—the last one, normally, in a softball competition—and she had seen no sign of trouble.

Maybe the next attempt on Janna's life wasn't going to take place tonight. Better yet, now that Superman was in the mix, maybe there wouldn't even *be* a next attempt.

"What's the score?" she asked Jimmy. She'd been too wary of everyone and everything to pay much attention to such details.

"Ten to ten," he told her. "The red team's up, two outs, man on second. If they send him home, it's all over."

Lois looked at him. "And if they don't?"

"Extra innings."

Lois watched Janna stroll out of the dugout and take her position in the on-deck circle. At the same time, Lyle Crossland, one of the substitute players, strode up to the plate. Lyle scowled darkly as he eyed the pitcher.

Suddenly a loud droning filled the air. Everyone on the ball field looked around to see where it was coming from.

"Look! Up in the sky!" someone shouted.

Lois looked up. Past the glare of the lights illuminating the field, she could see a dark form against the greater darkness of the night sky. A moment later she realized it was this form that was producing the droning.

An aircraft? This wasn't anywhere near the usual airport approaches.

Panic hit everywhere at once. People started running toward the exits. As the plane came closer, some people screamed. Others took cover under the stands.

From across the river, a huge transport plane was coming in—too low to be legitimate. Either this was the biggest coincidence Lois had ever seen, or the terrorists were making their move—and on a grand scale.

Jimmy, meanwhile, had the presence of mind to start snapping pictures—but not to worry about his own skin. Lois pulled at his sleeve.

"Come on!" she cried, struggling to make herself heard over the roar of the plane. "We've got to get out of here!"

Before Jimmy could take her advice, the plane's

bay doors opened and a fleet of tiny one-man gliders flew out. Lois tugged harder as the gliders headed for the field. Finally Jimmy started to move.

But by then the air was sizzling with pencil-thin bolts of lurid energy originating from the noses of the gliders. Lasers, Lois thought frantically. The kind that could slice a person in two.

Suddenly Jimmy pulled her down. A heartbeat later, a laser cut its way through the air above her head, leaving a jagged scar in the hard plastic seats behind her.

"Thanks," she told him.

Lois didn't hear his response. They were off and running again. But before they could get very far, a descending glider cut off their escape route. If they kept going, they'd be sliced to bits by his laser.

Lois turned, searching for another way out. Gliders were dropping earthward all over the place.

Desperately, she looked for Clark. He was no longer on the third baseline, naturally. She took that as a good sign—one they all needed badly.

"Go for it," she whispered after him.

As soon as he saw the gliders emerge from the belly of the plane, long before they began skimming over the field with their laser guns ablaze, Clark knew this was a job for Superman. Confident that no one would be watching him, he dashed under the seats and changed into the Man of Steel.

He could hear cries of encouragement as he

took to the air. By then the gliders were circling lower, raking the field and the seats with shafts of red fury. The grass was scarred and singed, burning in long black streaks.

But that wasn't all he had to worry about. The plane itself had shot over the field, but now it was describing a tight circle in the air—one it wasn't really built for.

It's coming back, Superman realized. And its trajectory was even lower now—as if aiming to make a suicide crash into the stands, taking out all of the innocent reporters and Leighton employees along with it.

The assassins' plan was obvious. They hoped to distract him with the gliders long enough for the transport plane to get past him.

Superman had a decision to make, and quickly. Should he stop the plane or take on the gliders? He gritted his teeth.

The gliders, he told himself. They were the most immediate threat. He still had several seconds before the plane tore into the crowd.

Flying at a speed that even he found difficult to muster, Superman darted from one glider to another, smashing them to bits. Each time he destroyed one, he grabbed the pilot and deposited him safely on the ground.

All the while, he could hear the transport plane getting closer and closer. With a quick glance, his X-ray vision revealed that it was empty of human life—its course either remote controlled or computer programmed in advance.

Also, it was loaded with explosives.

Lasers struck him left and right, dazzling him with their ferocity but no match for his alien skin. Nor were the gliders a match for his Kryptonian strength.

With a blazing burst of speed, he caught up with the last glider just as it was bearing down on a knot of reporters. Clenching his hands into fists, he ripped right through it, sparing only the pilot.

There was no time to knock the killers out or bind them. He would have to leave that to the police and the FBI.

Without a moment to spare, Superman turned and launched himself in the direction of the diving plane. Aided by gravity, it was careening toward the eastern section of stands and all its occupants.

The Man of Tomorrow slammed into the plane less than a hundred feet from its target. He could feel himself being driven back by the force of its dive. Digging his fingers into the metal nose, he fought its crushing momentum, striving with every ounce of strength at his disposal.

Muscles on fire, tendons standing out in his neck like steel cords, Superman battled to slow the plane down. He groaned with the effort, teeth grating, refusing to give in.

But for all his straining, there was a single terrible instant when he thought that he might not have arrived in time.

Had it taken him too long to disable the gliders? Were the people in the stands doomed as a result?

No, he told himself, digging even deeper for extra power. He was Superman. These people, this city . . . it was under his protection. He wasn't going to let a bunch of madmen destroy a single precious life.

Less than twenty feet from the ground, the Man of Steel began to turn the tide. He stopped the plane in midair. Then, on account of the explosives inside, he began pushing it the other way.

Faster and faster he flew, driving the plane tail first back into the sky. Once he was certain it was high enough for those on the ground to escape the blast, he gave it one last shove and sent it hurtling high above the earth.

When the plane was a mile or two above him, the heavens lit up, a huge ball of red and orange flame erupting from inside the metal frame. A moment later came a long, rolling *boom* as the explosion ripped across the sky.

Descending, Superman could hear scattered cries of gratitude rising from the ruined softball field. Debris from the plane rained down like fireworks, chunks of hot metal sizzling and crackling as they fell harmlessly into the nearby river.

Superman sighed. He didn't ever want to have to cut it that close again.

Still crouching between bleacher benches, Lois watched Jimmy snapping pictures of Superman's heroics. She saw the explosion, a fiery blossom high in the night sky—a sign that once again the Man of Steel had saved the day.

Lois couldn't help smiling with satisfaction. No matter what the terrorists or anyone else threw at him, Superman seemed equal to the task.

She looked out on to the playing field. Janna Leighton, standing near the pitcher's mound, looked badly shaken as she stared up into the heavens.

For the first time, Lois actually felt sorry for Janna. She had meant well, she'd had the city's best interests at heart. But in her determination to help out, she had made an error in judgment. Only Superman's intervention had prevented the situation from turning into a real catastrophe.

As Lois started down the steps toward the playing field, she noticed that one of the hot dog vendors had left his case of wares on the ground and was walking toward the ball field. His back was to Lois, so she couldn't see his face, but he seemed to be headed in Janna's direction.

There was something about him—something about his posture or the way he moved—that alerted Lois to danger. That feeling was confirmed a moment later, when she saw the vendor reach under his white jacket and pull out a long-barreled pistol.

All of a sudden, she understood. The plane, the gliders . . . they were *both* diversions. This was the real attack, the one nobody expected.

Without really thinking about what she was doing, Lois started running toward the gunman. By then, he had crossed the third baseline and was closing steadily on his target.

Her heart pumping hard against her ribs, Lois

saw the vendor raise his gun and take aim. Janna, gazing up at the sky like everyone else, had no idea what was about to happen.

Frantically, Lois forced herself to run harder. To gather momentum. And to stretch out into a hard, flat dive, her body parallel to the ground. A dive that allowed her to tackle the assassin at the knees.

The gun went off—but his aim was ruined. It fired into the sky, a small belch of flame compared to the fireworks falling into the river.

Surprised, unable to keep his balance, the gunman collapsed to his knees. But he was far from finished. With a snarl, he turned and backhanded Lois, stunning her.

Then he pointed his weapon at her. Her last thought before he pulled the trigger was that her sacrifice had been for nothing; Janna would be next.

As Lois closed her eyes, the gun went off. But a moment later, she was still thinking, still breathing. Opening her eyes, she saw that the assassin was no longer in front of her.

He was hanging in midair about ten feet up, Superman's hand clenching his wrist. And the gun was safely in Superman's other hand.

Lois shivered with relief. When she thought about how close she had come to death . . .

A moment later, the Man of Steel lowered the "vendor" into the waiting arms of the police. He turned over the gun as well. Then he landed beside Lois.

"Are you all right?" he asked. His face was creased with concern.

She managed a smile. "Yeah, I . . . I think so," she said.

Past Superman, Lois saw the haggard figure of Janna Leighton. The heiress looked too shocked to speak, but managed to say, "Thank you."

The reporter was too drained to give her much of a response. But she nodded, as if to say, *You're welcome.*

Superman, who had watched the exchange, smiled at Lois. "I've got to go now," he whispered. "But I'll see you later. And when I do . . . no more secrets, I promise."

Lois smiled in return. That prospect alone was worth everything she'd been through.

With a whoosh, Superman leaped into the air and flew away. As he circled over the playing field, the people on the field and in the stands murmured their thanks.

Lois was one of them.

As Abu made his way with his men through the crowded Metropolis Airport, he found that he regretted many things.

He regretted his failure to destroy Janna Leighton and her dreams. He regretted his inability to avenge his son's death. And strangely, more than he would ever have imagined, he regretted that he would not see any baseball games for a while.

Their gate was up ahead. "I thought we were going straight home to Quarac," Hakeem whispered, as he glanced at his ticket. "This says our destination is Buenos Aires."

Abu stopped short in his tracks and turned to his comrade. "We are taking the long way home," he said, careful not to let his frustration show. If the other travelers saw how angry he was, it might arouse suspicion.

Hakeem was the one who had engineered the assault on the softball field. It was he whom Abu would ultimately hold responsible for its breakdown, once they returned to their own country.

After all, the leaders of their organization had poured a great deal of money into the attacks on Janna Leighton. They would want someone to blame.

But none of this had to be discussed right now. There would be plenty of time for reprimands and recriminations later.

Another of Abu's men drew up alongside him. "This departure is not necessary," he said in a low voice. "Even Superman can be dealt with if we put our minds to it. We are giving up too easily."

"I'd have to disagree with you there," said a voice from behind them.

Abu turned—and saw Superman standing before him, his arms folded across his chest. He had the audacity to smile.

The bearded man seethed with rage and confusion. "How did you—?"

"It took a bit of doing," Superman said casually, "but a clever friend of mine figured out where you were staying. Seems you used the name 'Mr. Brown' once too often. It was just a matter of time before she tracked down you and your henchmen."

Abu's head felt as if it were going to explode. "You will never win this struggle," he spat, no longer caring who might hear or notice him. "There will be more of us, and still more. You cannot stop us."

Superman regarded him narrowly for a moment. "Don't look now," he said, "but I already have. I don't think your organization is going to put any more resources into killing Janna Leighton—not while *I'm* around."

As Superman said this, Hakeem made his move.

Abu saw him reach inside his coat and withdraw the plastic pistol he had intended to smuggle on to the plane. Aiming at the bright red *S* on Superman's chest, Hakeem squeezed the trigger six times, emptying the chamber.

Nearby travelers screamed and ducked for cover as the gunshots exploded in the terminal. But there were no ricochets, no danger to them.

A moment later, Abu saw why. Opening his hands, Superman showed them all six bullets. They hadn't even so much as left a mark on his palms.

Then, in a flash, the Man of Steel disarmed Hakeem. "Don't you know it's dangerous to play with guns?" he said, no longer smiling.

Squeezing the weapon in Hakeem's hand, he reduced it to plastic fragments. Then he dropped the pieces to the floor and brushed his hands together.

"Now," Superman said, turning to Abu, "this game is over. I advise you to give yourselves up."

Abu looked past Superman and saw the squad of police rushing to the scene. He realized there was nothing else he could do. Any further resistance would only lead to embarrassment—and he'd had enough of that to last him a lifetime.

"Yes," he said. "We will surrender."

Hakeem shook his head vehemently. "No. We must fight to the—"

Abu stopped him with a glance. "It is over," he declared.

His comrade struggled with the idea—but not for long. By then, the police had arrived.

16

LOIS COULDN'T STOP STARING at Clark's face in the soft glow of the candlelight.

They were seated at a table in a far corner of the Cossack Tea Room, as far away from the other patrons as they could get. Clark reached for her hands and took them in his.

"So," she said, "do I get my explanation now?"

"You mean the one you so richly deserve?" he asked.

Lois nodded. "Yes, that one."

"Well," Clark replied, "it's simple, really—in a way. First, let me emphasize again that at no time was I romantically interested in Janna Leighton."

Lois looked at him askance. "Not even for a second?"

He smiled. "I'm serious. There's no one in my

life but you, and there never will be. I want you to know that."

She drew the moment out a little longer, then let him off the hook. "I know," she said. "And deep down, I never had any doubt of it. But I still don't understand why—"

"I'm getting to that," Clark assured her. "Actually, it started out as a pretty routine story. I'd heard a rumor that with Alexander Leighton gone, the family was going to sell the Monarchs— maybe even move them to another city. So I wangled an interview with his daughter."

"At some romantic rendezvous?" Lois gibed, unable to resist.

He looked at her. "At her office, to be perfectly accurate. That's when I realized that someone was after her. You see, there was a man on a scaffold outside her office, washing windows. He didn't look like he was doing a very good job, so when Janna wasn't looking, I scanned him with my X-ray vision."

"He was armed?" she guessed.

Clark nodded. "He had a high-powered pistol underneath his coveralls. It didn't take much to figure out what he was up to. But there was neither time nor opportunity for me to change into Superman."

Lois leaned forward. "How did you stop him?"

"When he pulled the gun out, I slipped my glasses down and used my heat vision to burn one of the ropes holding up the scaffolding. He had on a safety belt, so I knew he wouldn't fall—and I wouldn't have to find a way to catch him.

"Janna called the police, and they got there a

few minutes later. All they had to do was open the window and haul the guy in."

"So you knew right away you were on to more than just a Monarchs story," Lois observed. "Why didn't you go to press with it right away?"

"Because the FBI showed up," Clark explained. "They told me there was a terrorist conspiracy to assassinate Janna—but that if the story got out, there would be a panic. People are concerned enough about terrorists as it is. If they thought they were right here in Metropolis . . . "

"I get the idea," she told him. "But—"

"Why couldn't I tell you about it?" he asked, anticipating her question. He shook his head. "They swore me to secrecy, Lois—no exceptions. They asked me to keep a lid on the whole thing until they had arrested everyone involved." He appealed to her with his eyes. "Don't you see? I gave them my *word*."

Finally Lois understood the magnitude of Clark's dilemma. Thanks to his upbringing in Smallville, he was a man who believed in old-fashioned virtues. A man for whom honesty was more than a word.

And yet, ever since he'd come to Metropolis, he'd been forced to live a white lie—to cover up the fact that Clark Kent was Superman. That forced him to stretch the truth a lot, despite what he'd been taught.

Then some federal official had asked him to keep quiet about a delicate investigation, where lives were at stake. Clark had to choose between breaking his word to that official and letting his fiancée in on the secret. And given the fact that she didn't *have* to know . . .

"You get it?" he asked hopefully.

"I think so," Lois told him. "At least, the first part. And your spending time with Janna? I'm to believe that that was to protect her?"

"To tell the truth," he replied, "I probably could have done that just as well watching her from afar. The problem was, Janna offered me the scoop of the year—an exclusive insider's view of what it was like to be stalked by terrorists. As a reporter, I'd have raised a lot of eyebrows by turning that down. And a fellow like me," he said pointedly, "can't afford to be raising too many eyebrows."

Lois got it now. She got it only too well. After all, she'd seen the first of Clark's articles on the subject. As he'd said, it just *might* be the scoop of the year.

Besides, hadn't she made the same kind of deal with Slam Bradley? And the detective was only acting on his own, not even aware of the FBI investigation. Of course, her story—about the boatyard's involvement in the murder scheme— paled beside Clark's.

But that was okay. She didn't mind someone else getting the limelight for a change—as long as it was only once in a while.

Clark smiled. "So you understand, right? I mean, I'm sorry I had to withhold all this from you. But under the circumstances, I didn't have any choice."

Lois sighed. "Okay. I forgive you, especially

since that honesty of yours works both ways. I'll never have to worry about you seeing another woman on the sly."

"Never," he echoed.

"You know," said Lois, "maybe these past few days weren't such a bad thing after all."

Clark looked at her, surprised. "How's that?"

She squeezed his hand. "It's reminded me just how much you mean to me."

Obviously her fiancé liked the sound of that. He leaned forward a little more, no doubt meaning to kiss her. But for some reason he stopped short and looked past her.

Lois turned to follow his gaze. She groaned.

It was Janna Leighton, striding up to them in another knockout dress. And she had Steve Lombard, the TV news reporter, hooked on to her arm.

"Speak of the devil," Lois whispered.

"Clark," said Janna, obviously delighted to see him. "And Lois Lane. Imagine meeting you here."

Yes, thought Lois, *imagine a reporter being able to afford this place. Even two reporters going Dutch.*

Janna had obviously recuperated from her latest brush with death. Her smile was as easy as it was attractive.

The heiress looked at Clark. "I just wanted to say thank you," she told him, "for all your help these last few days. I mean it."

Leaning forward, she kissed him on each cheek. Then she turned to Lois.

"And you, Miss Lane. I can't tell you how grateful I

am that you saw that gunman—and that you stopped him." She chuckled. "That was quite a tackle."

Lois shrugged. "He didn't see it coming."

"They never do," Janna remarked.

Lois still thought Janna was standing just a little too close to Clark for comfort, but she told herself not to react. The woman was just here to say thanks and leave, and that was all.

"I'm just glad it's over," Clark said, glancing at Lois. He raised his hand to the side of his head and rubbed it as though it were still tender. "I don't think I'll be doing any sailing in the near future."

"Why, you were a terrific sailor," Janna told him. "And a terrific roller skater, too." Suddenly her expression sobered. "But it's not over yet. Not by a long shot."

Lois looked at her, surprised. She could see that Clark had tensed up, too, no doubt wondering what the heiress meant by that.

"There's still that small matter of Quarac," Janna noted. "I already have my people checking into the situation over there. It seems my father handed those people a raw deal. I've got a lot of work ahead of me if I'm going to make it up to them."

Clark seemed to relax. "That strikes me as a good idea," he said.

Janna's smile returned. "I will miss you," she told Clark.

The heiress turned to Lois again. "You know, you're a very lucky woman, Miss Lane. But then, Clark's a lucky man. I feel better knowing I'm 'losing' him to someone like you."

Lois acknowledged the compliment. "Thanks. I appreciate that." *But you never had him to "lose,"* she thought.

"Well," Janna said, straightening. "Steven and I don't want to be late for the opera. Do we, Steve?"

"No," Lombard said cheerfully. "You've got to love that *La Bohemian*."

"*La Bohème*," Janna corrected.

Lombard shrugged good-naturedly. "Whatever."

Saying their good-byes, the heiress and her date left Lois and Clark alone again. Lois turned to the man in her life.

"I'll tell you this much," she said. "You may not have been interested in Janna, but she was definitely interested in *you*."

Clark looked at her. "No way," he replied.

"Absolutely," Lois insisted. "A woman knows these things."

Her companion thought about it, then shook his head. "Come on, Lois. We were just on the same team for a while. That's all it ever was for either of us."

"If that's what you want to believe . . ." Lois told him.

She reached across the table. Her hands covered his.

"I mean, just look at *us*," she said, drawing closer to him. "We started out as teammates, too. And look where *we* wound up."

About the Author

When roused from one of his frequent and enduring daydreams of a world where baseball players never go on strike and White Castle hamburgers grow on trees, M. J. Friedman will admit to being the author of nineteen science fiction and fantasy books, among them a great many Star Trek and Star Trek: The Next Generation bestsellers.

When he's not writing—a condition that lately occurs with the frequency of Halley's Comet—Friedman enjoys sailing, jogging, and spending time with his adorable wife Joan and equally adorable clones . . . er, sons. He's quick to note that no matter how many Friedmans you may know, he's probably not related to any of them.